I0738453

Pathway to the Stars:
Part 1, Vesha Celeste

Author – Matthew J. Opdyke

Title – Pathway to the Stars

Subtitle – Part 1, Vesha Celeste

Publisher – FTB Pathway Publications

Copyright © Matthew J. Opdyke, 2019

All Rights Reserved

IngramSpark 5 x8

Glossy Paperback Edition

ISBN – 978-05784362-3-4

Matthew J. Opdyke

Disclaimers

This is a work of science fiction and utopian fantasy. The names, characters, businesses, places, incidents, locales, and events are either the products of the author's imagination or used in a fictitious way and with the utmost of respect toward all parties.

Reading this text and enjoying it may take you on a journey that is enjoyable while increasing your reading comprehension level as well as your philosophical and creative literacy. If there are any blatant errors or constructive suggestions, please advise the author through email, at:

info@mjopublications.com

This book was written using the mind and heart of the author, and in many cases, it was written completely "off the grid." In brief moments if there is a quote, the author uses quotations and directly sites the author within the text. In many occasions, the author wrote prose and phrases that are spoken every day, or in the past, and should never be taken from any artist since a major part of any amazing story brings a sense of normalcy. Otherwise, this text is original in every sense, wherein, in this book the author also suggests we search for the well-being of those around us as well as ourselves.

Table of Contents

Epigraph

"Each one of you can change the world,

For you are made of star stuff,

And you are connected to the Universe."

~ Vera Cooper Rubin,

Astronomer

~ * ~

"Somewhere, something incredible

is waiting to be known.

~ Carl Sagan

~ * ~

"There may be obstacles,

but there are no limits."

~ Mark Dean,

Computer Engineer

Preface by Author

This is the first in the Booklet Series titled "Pathway to the Stars." Let's journey together and get to know Vesha Celeste and a few other amazing characters as they reveal the details of this space opera. The first book in "Pathway to the Stars," the series, is about "Vesha Celeste."

This story is intended to afford everyone in this worldwide audience a chance to read and ponder on many edifying words as our heroes engage to overcome the various obstacles through life. What they do, say, and achieve is intended to bring hope to our hearts and help our minds. This series is designed to allow each of us to flourish with peaceful ideals. This will allow us to consider all factors, challenging or fun, while we foment our creativity, ingenuity, and innovation, and shift our focus toward positive pursuits, setting in motion a beautiful future where space-travel throughout the Universe is involved.

Getting there can start with the simple things. A humble smile and a hello to passers-by, gracious words to those who help, helping someone pick up those spilt groceries, for example, with no thought for reward, and simply being kind will bring joy to our lives, especially as we reach out to others in the spirit of love, compassion, and wisdom. I believe that as difficult as it may seem at times, we can find joy in searching for the good in others, as we allow them to inspire the greatness within us too, just as we do this for them.

Furthermore, it is up to each of us to ensure we as a civilization can study the various sciences in-depth, maximize our potential, whether through music, art, science, or genuine service to others, so we can build a legacy that is deemed worthy of preserving for the long-haul. Our potential is ours, so let's be amazing.

Each moment is worth every journey taken. I am sure that as you embrace these stories and meet these characters, if you don't already, you too will believe that political, fantasy, and utopian science fiction are tools for ideas to be shared in a way that will inspire greatness. Fantasy, with idealism and hope for the better part of our nature, humanity, and future, can create a pleasant environment that entertains us, strengthens us, and takes us away into a reality that further encourages our great minds to do many more great things. Letting go and writing this part of the grand space odyssey has filled my days with wonder and hope. Using many of my own rules and considering ideas for an enriching and a healthy state of mind with a penchant for innovation has invigorated my resolve to move forward no matter the obstacles we face.

In this part of the larger story, the issue of gender-discrimination is addressed. Innocence of mind with an appreciation for the beauty of our bodies and our minds, and a desire to understand our Universe more fully, are expressed through Vesha Celeste, Sky, Eliza Williams, Yesha Alevtina, and many of her other friends. I have allowed these characters the ability to invent and benefit from the "awesomest" technologies that are only in our dreams.

The characters in this story required specific tools and environmental aspects to overcome difficult challenges, many of which we can conceive of at this time in our history. This story occurs in a timeframe much like our own. Amuse yourself reading this story as our heroes face their obstacles fearlessly and still find plenty of time and means to make life exciting and fun.

My goals here revolve around a future where each of us, accepting our choices for longevity and respecting the choices of others to maintain their way of being in a more natural state, can live in harmony.

As our friends traverse the Universe, it would be nice to greet them when they return. However, many may opt to have future generations do that, and that my friends, is their choice to make, at least until their children reach the legal age to choose for themselves. Space-faring individuals will need the ability to buffet against all the various challenges we confront and environments we face in space. Sciences, arts, industries of medicine and health, educational and correctional systems, our solar system, intergalactic travel, and stepping back from time to time to ask how, why, what, and then deciding when, are all necessary components of a promising future. Enjoy!

~ Matthew J. Opdyke, Author

Chapter 01: A Memorial

Database Moon Archive, Celestial-Sol Entry Date: 2018 December 25. The following is an excerpt from a private speech and presentation about Vesha Celeste preceding implementation of a new advancement inside Pathway's covert campus. Database Moon Archive input made by Yesha Alevtina, President of Pathway Industries, from 2015-2022.

"Notwithstanding her dedication to her craft, Vesha Celeste loved, taught, mentored, and raised her children in an enriching environment. She nurtured them until they, just as she, expressed their own genius and doctoral interests. Throughout her life there seemed to be beautiful dreams filled with amazing journeys, dreams that Vesha had hoped would eventually spring into reality. In the real world, she maintained firm footing in topics she found intriguing and honorable. She raised her children to demonstrate their beauty of expertise so that they could leave behind them a history replete with their own legacies. She wrote books for the masses about galaxies, our Universe, and dark matter. She wrote to her grandchildren about how their grandmother was an astronomer and a dreamer. What hadn't dawned on her was the fact that she had so much more potential than she had ever realized in the almost nine decades that she lived. Whether she had untold potential or had reached that state of self-actualization, her contributions were more than could be asked of anyone. Vesha shared her love of the Universe with many. She wrote to edify not only those closest to her but people all over the world. She wrote to enlighten and help us to understand and gain an interest in the many wonders yet to be found and understood throughout our grand Universe. She inspired many to pursue their dreams and to do so with purpose in their lives while living with confidence. She taught people to never shy away from the truth as evidenced in science, or from faith as this too had tempered her passions in life. No matter her journeys, her compassion for others continuously grew."

Yesha Alevtina, President of Pathway, was sharing her thoughts regarding her dear friend, Vesha. In so doing, she stood proudly deliberating before those in attendance at the Pathway Convention Center, two years after her passing. Yesha continued.

"It was the evening of December 25th, 2016, when Vesha's spirit left this world, but many visions stood before her, yet to be realized. Some of those dreams will begin today, and some will not be recognized for many years to come. Soon we will watch as a miracle of genius occurs and moves the blessings of the sands of time to a reality allowing us to connect to and save even more lives.

"Much has been said, and much may yet be told regarding her work and her journey. I, Yesha, am merely a young friend who loves her dearly. As I relay her story, I am doing so with the advantages of neuroscience and the ability to see what many may not. Vesha's never-ending struggle for education, her clarity about understanding our Universe, and her tenacity to thrive in a professional field despite being turned away in her youth are examples of her resilience. Even in her later years, due to our shared and unfortunate mortality, she was denied the opportunity of becoming a Nobel Laureate. Her vast impact on science and each one of us will not go unnoticed by any of us here today. She was inspiring to so many, including to myself. She is a testament that we should never betray humanity by silencing more than half of our human potential. We should never dare to silence anyone for that matter. We reveal our purpose and our character with the love emanating from our words and resultant actions. We should never find ourselves dismissing the staggering breadth of our shared mental capacity, nor should we alienate so many great individuals who would otherwise be extraordinary, if given the opportunity to fully blossom. This will be our opportunity to grant a fuller potential that will bless each of our lives in remarkable ways.

"Vesha was dedicated to her craft while respecting her personal beliefs. She balanced her respect for the truths found in science and her love of her children and grandchildren. Her virtues drew me in to honor her within the story I will share with each of you. I will share with you how a series of dynamic events has brought us all where we are now. Perhaps one day this story will be shared with many generations on many planets throughout the Universe and beyond. This journey and how it began may take us on an enjoyable and a promising pathway to the stars. With enough hope, vision, and action we will enjoy many potentially amazing voyages throughout the cosmos. Today, I will, in the most respectful way, cast Vesha in the favorable light she deserves. This hard-to-believe perspective was recorded from her mind during the last hour before she passed.

"Filled with fantasy and speculation to some who come upon this story in a different reality, you know now that without her we would not be where we are today. Today we are on the precipice of human history, longevity sciences, and readying to span the cosmos.

"Please journey with me on this presentation of her life, beginning just two years prior."

Chapter 02: The Ebb of Life

Database Moon Archive, Celestial-Sol Entry Date: 2018 December 25. The following is a brief biography, narrated by Yesha Alevtina, and shown via a holograph presentation, during a speech about Vesha Celeste to Pathway citizens within the Pathway Covert Campus. Database Moon Archive input made by Yesha Alevtina, President of Pathway Industries, from 2015-2022.

It was late in the evening of December 25, 2016. After keying up music from Gabriel Yared's score for the movie, "Message in a Bottle," Vesha fluffed her pillow. She yearned to meet the angel who had accompanied her during her dreams throughout life. As she and her dream angel healed hearts and minds, they forged the bond of understanding between many, no matter where they went. Vesha turned the covers to lay propped up on her bed and drifted to thoughts of the beautiful day spent with her family. Having gazed upon photos of her daughter, Jillian Yenn, and her husband,

Ralston Rayna, she thought of each of her family members while placing her smartphone on her dresser.

She contemplated on her own life and how, from her perspective, the time had actually been pretty good to her. As she did, Vesha felt overwhelmed by the beauty and wonder of it all. Vesha's final moments would pass soon, she knew that. Soon, she would embrace a sweet new reality. Perhaps this time she would journey with her life's fanciful dream angel, but first, she felt the need to think of her past and present, a habit she picked up from a much younger, but dear friend when she first talked about it twenty-two years ago. When Vesha would reflect on her experiences, she would consider her real-life happenings, what she could learn or appreciate from them, and then ponder upon her visions, before she would submit to the future. It had been a couple of prolonged and somewhat challenging years since her lovely daughter, Jillian, had passed away. Several years before Jillian's passing, her honorable, knowledgeable, supporting, and loving husband, Ralston, had gone on his journey to the afterlife as well.

"*Oh, how I miss them both.*" She paused.

"*I wish they were here now,*" she thought as she felt her emotions loom and swell.

"*Perhaps there will be plenty of time for exploration and discovery with those I love in the next part of my reality. Perhaps there is more to all that we* know than we understand now. Yes, we're only beginning to comprehend the complexity of it all. There is certainly room for a fuller understanding of our Universe. It would be nice to hold on to this reality and find a day we can share a heartwarming existence with other civilizations throughout the cosmos. We'll see..." Vesha certainly had a hope of something more significant.

Pondering upon that which brought her peace of mind, Vesha felt comfortable with the contributions she had made to the world. She had brought clarity to the understanding of dark matter achievements in science, but she was more intrigued by the delightful people who had been a unique part of her life. No matter her grasp of the seemingly sane, she admired this beautiful angel who graced each stage of her life and who glowed with iridescent colors imperceptible to many. She had been there in benevolence within her dreams throughout her eighty-eight years in her own unique, somewhat extraordinary and sometimes normal-seeming, and yet unusual journey. She had met many brilliant people. Still, she wished she could reach many more, but life as she understood it came with a beginning and an end. Her two dear and young friends, Eliza and Yesha, had assured her that science within Pathway Industries had come with an opportunity to continue on. She could continue life in a healed and optimized state, as an immortal. Knowing those truths, she decided to lend herself to science and let them do their best, but only as she went to her rest first, as her God had planned. If her God saw fit to bring her back to this mortal realm, she would accept that.

A night-light had been installed, so when she looked up at her ceiling, a giant mural of the Andromeda Galaxy lay above her within her field of view. It seemed to glow after she reached behind her nightstand to turn the light switch to the off position. Again, she repositioned herself, this time settling on her back to lay to rest. As she put her head on her pillow, she sighed.

She had taken residency within the Princeton Assisted Living Facility, due to suffering from various stages of dementia. Luckily, the facility and her family gifted her with the ability to look up at the Andromeda Galaxy mural on her ceiling each night. Doing so brought her a sense of normalcy. Vesha marveled at the blessings of her own life with pause and gratitude. She embraced the rich complexities of love and reflected upon the miracles of experience. She contemplated upon her pursuits of happiness and the gifts her faith had given her as it tempered her fervor toward the complexities of science. She felt as though truth lay somewhere within both, or quite possibly between the two. Perhaps science and faith were merely portions of the truth. Maybe the answers to everything were scattered and hidden in places yet to be discovered.

The tug of the Universe beckoned.

She began to drift and think about the intricate details of her life – this day, in particular, had been perfect. The visit had gone as planned; the weather outside had been clear; the evening had been perfect for viewing the nighttime sky. Quite warm for winter, it had been 49° Fahrenheit and had turned into an evening of delight shared with clear skies, a very slight crescent Moon, and lovely company. With one last gaze of the Universe and one final and fascinating view of the stars, nebula, and galaxies using her Orion SkyQuest XT10 Classic Dobsonian Telescope, installed on the balcony outside the sliding door of her living quarters, she found herself endlessly impressed as she scanned in the directions of Cassiopeia, Orion, and back to Andromeda. It had been given to Vesha for her eighty-fifth birthday by her daughter, who had discovered a month after Vesha's birthday that she had terminal cancer, and sadly passed away just six months later. Enjoying this gift from her sweet and thoughtful daughter, Vesha knew there was yet so much for humanity to understand, and so much further that civilization could go. *"Maybe she is flying in Heaven with my dream angel. Maybe she is with Ralston, playing a game of golf in some other Universe."*

Returning to what she knew was reality and contemplating the mechanics of such a fine and modern instrument, Vesha had used many powerful telescopes before, observed deep into the Universe, and made many scientific journal entries, but this one was special, it was not only a gift from Jillian, but it had demonstrated to her how far science had advanced. In her younger days, it took buildings the size of a home to see what she could see with this small telescope, just about as tall as she, with its capabilities—abilities that were similar to those she had found in professional observatories from her younger years. She was glad that now this was available to so many young and aspiring astronomers today. *"Maybe they will develop something that can be shared with the public that will afford everyone the opportunity to see with more clarity and detail the planets of our Galaxy, and within the galaxies just this side of the cosmic microwave background. Perhaps, they'll be able to derive the full complexity of our Universe, someday."*

Vesha had made an effort to stargaze every clear night, since the doctors had told her that due to her condition, stargazing would help her to stay grounded, triggering memories of critical experiences and influential people and ideas in her life.

Family and friends had visited Vesha where she was staying for the Christmas and Hanukkah holiday festivities in Princeton, New Jersey. Missing among those that attended were her daughter and husband; for them, the beautiful flicker of light had faded away—gone the way of the wind leaving behind them the wispy smoke of distant memories and unforgettable greatness of their lives. Her children, Daniel, Chris, and Avery, her five grandchildren, including Jillian's daughter, Lara, and her great-granddaughter had gathered with her friends, Eliza, Yesha, Najem, Jasmine, James, Amber, and Erin to celebrate the festivities together and this visit had been one of the most wonderfully charming parts of the season. Despite minor frustrations and lapses in memory, Vesha recalled quite pleasantly the holiday greetings exchanged, the stories told, and the smiles shared. To her, life had been lived to its fullest, and she felt that her pursuit of happiness had been blessed with a pleasant bookend; this was home. Her family had sung songs, they had exchanged gifts, and everyone had reminisced upon life's adventurous journeys and fondest memories—her domicile was still decorated for both Christmas and Hanukkah, and the scent of pine, holiday spices, and the smoke of blown out candles lingered in the air. Vesha had given and received goodbye hugs and kisses from those who she felt closest to throughout life.

Matthew J. Opdyke

Chapter 03: Her Early Days

Database Moon Archive, Celestial-Sol Entry Date: 2018 December 25. The following is the continuation of a brief biography, also narrated by Yesha Alevtina, and shown via a holograph presentation, where Vesha Celeste combs back into the deeper recesses of her mind despite her dementia to think back to those earlier days of her parents, before birth, and on through to college. This Database Moon Archive input was made by Yesha Alevtina, President of Pathway Industries, from 2015-2022.

As Vesha Celeste continued to contemplate, she began to find herself drifting away from the affairs of the day to the very beginning of her life. Her Father, Lukas, had emigrated from Lithuania to the United States and had changed his last name from Petrauskas to Celeste more than a century ago. Life in that part of the world was difficult and still ravaged by the existence of various civil wars. Her Mother, born Irena

Cara, had been an American immigrant from what is now known as Moldova, in the early 1900s, since antisemitism was on the rise in that region, with stories of murders within the newspapers of the day, and all-too-often. Lukas and Irena were both Jewish immigrants in those early days and despite all, they shared a fascination for science. As life took its course, they both found each other and fell in love in Philadelphia while working together at Bell Telephone, until their marriage shortly after.

Her father continued to work at Bell as an electrical engineer, yet because of specific workplace rules that existed in the US during those days, only one family member could work there at a time. Luckily, with the Celeste's first child on her way, Irena did her best to prepare for their newborn, and had more time to do so with reduced stress. Vesha's older sister, Evelina Celeste, came into this world first, and just as it would be for Vesha in the years that followed, Evelina was raised well. Later on, in Evelina's life, she rose above the social and gender politics of the day and became an Administrative Judge for the US Department of Defense—an honor deserving of its own story.

On a lovely day in Philadelphia, Pennsylvania, July 23, in the year of 1928, Vesha Florence Celeste came into this world. Her parents had shared with her many times how beautiful that summer day was, which had made the experience an unforgettably pleasant memory—

they never failed to remind Vesha of how adorable she was as a little baby girl.

"You were beautiful, smiling, and a saint if I ever saw one," both of her parents told her, as she grew older and was filled with questions.

While she couldn't remember more than vicarious details about that experience, she wistfully and fleetingly recalled the memories of her journeys with her beautiful dream angel in those younger years, as well as the Celeste's move to Washington, DC, when she was ten years old.

Washington, DC in 1938 had an air of hope; it was teaming with genius minds, the arts and entertainment industries were in full bloom, and Vesha had become entranced by astronomy. The home base of a bustling and free country, full of vim and vigor, had added to how much it was that she fancied the breaks she would take from her studies during each day. During these breaks she would contemplate her dreams of the stars and ponder on what was out there so far away and just beyond our abilities to see. Vesha had looked forward to each night for years and became ensconced for hours merely gazing upon the stars as they sped by. Her mother would catch her doing so quite routinely, but she knew she did it to stay awake while doing her studies.

Nevertheless, Mrs. Celeste would tell Vesha, "Don't stay up all night hanging out by the window."

When Vesha was done with her lessons, she would rest and go on more journeys of love and honor, with her friend of deep-thought, an angel she named Sky. No matter her dreams, she kept them private and carried herself embracing the reality of each day.

Her father, Lukas, continued to cultivate his daughter's love for the cosmos and began to take her to science and astronomy conventions regularly. These conventions, in the heart of DC, was where she, in 1940 and only thirteen years old, met Najem Grace for the first time, who was fifteen years old. Najem had moved to Baltimore with her family, and shortly thereafter she wasted no time and put together another one of her many astronomy clubs. If there were one or two people who frequented her clubs, that was fine with Najem; it was nice to be in the company of other curious minds.

When they first met each other, Vesha's new friend, Najem, had traveled to Washington, DC to enjoy some of the university conventions. The world of physics in all of its forms was expanding and understanding how the mechanisms that governed the Universe and how it worked was exciting to an increasing segment of society, as well as to both of these two young and beautiful friends.

Since Vesha and Najem were both young ladies, the two youngest members of the audience, and had so much in common they quickly warmed up to each other's love of all things related to space and the future and became pen-pals for life. Together, they spent many hours with each other every couple of weeks for more than two years during their visits, talking about the stars and how to improve the quality of life. After Najem finished high school, however, they rarely had an opportunity to see each other. Even though life kept them apart, they still wrote letters and eagerly sent them in the mail. They looked forward to their correspondence with each other, hoped for return letters, and were never disappointed.

Two years after moving to DC, in 1942, Mr. Celeste, who had mentored, taught, and inspired her—proud of her love of science, helped her build her first telescope to peer out into the heavens. Vesha wasted no time that first and glorious evening, taking her telescope out to the small backyard and peering up into the sky. *"Fitting,"* she thought, *"no wonder I named my angel, Sky."* She pondered a moment and then continued to gaze into the sky again.

Vesha was tickled silly, since the night was clear. She happened to peer north to see Cassiopeia and Andromeda, with Sagittarius in view to the southeast, with its bright glow of stars climbing up high and into the sky at a sixty-degree angle, where it met the Orion Spur and the Perseus Arm. She contemplated the position of the Earth's revolution around the Sun, compared to our point and place within our newly-understood galaxy, the Milky Way, and knew that by looking through the bright arms of stars, she was looking into the galactic disc. Looking over at the teapot asterism of Sagittarius also gave her reference to the galactic north and south poles. She enjoyed having clarity on those details, and she had her parents, Najem, one school teacher, and Sky to thank for it.

While her home environment was supportive, a couple of years later, as high school was reaching its finality for Vesha, life became somewhat dynamic. Her parents had reinforced her efforts throughout her life. However, when her professors asked what she planned to do following her graduation, giving an honest and sincere answer about her interest in studying science, she was rebuked. She remembered how she had confided with one professor about her plans to study astronomy in college and how she had planned on pursuing that as a profession. Her science teacher, despite hearing as she confidently shared her hopes, her intentions, and her dreams, and having full knowledge of her incredible work ethic, as well as the dedication demonstrated through her studies, scholastics, and award-winning academic achievements, dismissively responded, "You'll do alright so long as you stay away from science."

She remembered that day how she came home a bit taken back, a bit perplexed, and a little out of sorts. *"Was this how things were going to be for women in science? Would more than half our human potential be silenced in the name of societal norms?"* she thought.

Both of her parents picked up on her emotional cues and asked her what had happened, listened to her, and then lovingly reminded her that she could do anything that she put her mind to. "You should never let another individual destroy your hopes, your dreams, or your resolve," her mother told her. Her parents encouraged her to write to her friend, Najem, who was studying astronomy in college at the time, and let her know what had happened. Perhaps Vesha wasn't alone in the duplicities of society. She had talked to her parents during many dinner meals about how Najem had struggled to be able to study science as a young woman too. Mr. and Mrs. Celeste shared with Vesha that they felt it honorable from their point of view that she desired to continue putting her hopes in the starry night sky, and that she should not allow her spirits to dampen.

Her parents loved and supported Vesha through her studies because that was her wish, that was what she wanted to do, that was what inspired her, and they trusted and loved her decisions for her future, no matter her choices. Vesha had demonstrated and proved to them on many occasions and for many years that she could excel in and would be an asset to the science community or any field of study that she put her mind to.

That night, before falling asleep, she had thought about what her parents had said and had appreciated them for their support, their kindness, and their love. As she drifted into her dreams, there was Sky, her dream angel, heralding her along, engaging in heroic acts of daring-do, and letting her know, *"Your dreams are yours to pursue, they are beautiful, and you can't let anyone slow you down."*

As her years in high school drew to a close, Lukas and Irena continued to mentor Vesha on setting personal goals, developing her own code of ethics, and being driven from within by her own guiding standards. They had motivated her intrigues for many years, by providing an enriching environment that would cause her curiosity in the sciences to blossom; she had been in a setting that had balanced her spiritual life with her ambitions for a career, which in turn fomented her dedication toward understanding the beauty and complexities of her Universe. Her father had reminded her that when he signed her up for membership in that advanced science program for youth almost four years ago, the place where she had met Najem, she would come home and share the exciting developments and discoveries as revealed by the professors, the faculty, and the scientists. He assured her that he had taken her to these meetings regularly, because he had great hope in her and in her potential for a positive impact on life, on science, and on society. He told her that she would burn bright no matter the challenge.

The struggles for equality for women in science were pretty rampant in the US in those days, as were similar unfortunate circumstances throughout the world. In addition to the bustle of society that brought her joy through her younger years, the world was significantly impacted by surrounding droughts and economic shortfalls. Adding to that era, were the events of the 1930s and the 1940s—the tragedies and the toll of the effects of the great depression, wars, and the toxicity prevalent in the minds of those who sought to harm others for no reason that could suitably justify the sacrifice of their lives. Notwithstanding, Vesha focused her energies on meaningful conquests by scraping together beat up old materials from 19th-century telescopes—much like her friend, Najem would have done, and occupy her time repairing them. She would challenge herself to defy her school counselors by focusing on astronomy with that field of study driving her sites in college.

Vesha graduated from high school in 1944 and never wavered in her pursuit of a career in science; *"No one can take my dreams away if I stay focused and dedicated,"* she recalled.

Chapter 04: Love & Intellect

Database Moon Archive, Celestial-Sol Entry Date: 2018 December 25. The following is the continuation of a brief biography, also narrated by Yesha Alevtina, and shown via a holograph presentation, where Vesha Celeste combs back into the deeper recesses of her mind despite her dementia to think back to those earlier days of college and meeting her husband, Ralston. This Database Moon Archive input was made by Yesha Alevtina, President of Pathway Industries, from 2015-2022.

Through her studies, Vesha had built a collection of many favorite contemporaries. One of her favorites, Maria Mitchell, had been the first female astronomy professor in US history at Vassar College for Women, in 1865. Maria had also been the first American to be recognized worldwide as an astronomer. This brazen and profoundly-smart lady had, following years of research and dedication, discovered a comet in the nighttime skies above the US in the 1800s. Vesha had chosen to attend this college, and she too spent many hours combing the cosmos with her shrewd telescope at home, as well as the more robust telescopes on campus. The comparisons ran thick, and it inspired Vesha. As the only astronomy major in her graduating class, she persisted in her studies as she combed over physics, math, and her other core curriculum. A deeper understanding of her lessons and perseverance led to Vesha's graduation with an induction to Phi Beta Kappa—the oldest-known honor society for the liberal arts and sciences in the US.

After Vassar, Vesha was in full spirits and anxiously applied for the graduate astrophysics program at Princeton University. Again, she found controversy. Contemplating on the state of the day, Vesha opined.

"With the expectations that existed, I knew how things were, and I was aware of the social norms, but I valued astronomy, my goals, and an excellent education—my parents raised me well by supporting me and my life-enriching choices. Still, it's just as important to stay strong and step forward with hope and might," Vesha recalled, speaking to her angel, named Sky, in a quiet conversation within her mind.

Princeton, which happened to be one of the first colleges of the original thirteen colonies of the US, and was now a university, did not send her a graduate catalog in time for enrollment that year and they wouldn't mail one soon enough or any time within the foreseeable future.

"They were caught up in the sentiments and cultural norms of the time, but fortunately many years later they came around," she recalled and graciously forgave them. At that time in history, Princeton women were not allowed in science programs, at least not until 1975.

"Just as well," she thought to herself, as she reflected on the events that ensued shortly after. The first day, following her bus ride to campus, after being accepted to study at Cornell University, in Ithaca, NY, something wonderful happened. *"Good things came because of it,"* Vesha pondered. She met her life-long love, Ralston Rayna.

Ralston had been sent to Cornell by the United States Navy to study chemical engineering. Vesha had enrolled there as well in both physics and astrophysics. She recalled her discussions later on, following her studies through the days, the weeks, and the months that followed, with him, and how they shared an affinity for science.

To Vesha, their discussions were intriguing and surprising. She recalled what Ralston said on their first trip to the local park, following a very philosophical conversation, *"Perhaps the efforts of great scientists to understand humanity and the Universe will help solve more problems that plague the well-being of so many throughout the world than the currently accepted status quo."*

As it would happen for any individual with at least a tender attachment to their personal nature, young love was not uncommon in those days. Vesha remembered how, not too long after she and Ralston met, their sentiments toward each other had brewed to an intense boil, *"It was the good kind of boiling, Sky, you know, the kind that when making confectionary treats for fun, sweet caramel and chocolatey desserts are the result. Yes, it was quite the blessing meeting Ralston."*

Vesha even recalled blissfully how little time it took for them to confide in each other the reality of how attracted they were and for more reasons than physical appeal alone. Although, there was that too.

Having grown into a lovely young lady with dark hair, kind blue eyes, and a cheerful and intellectual disposition, she was soon acutely aware that hers was also a disposition very striking to Ralston, *"He let me know in so many ways throughout my life how much joy I brought to him. His feelings were reciprocated in kind since he brought so much joy to my life; I saw in him a tall, handsome, charismatic, and very considerate and knowledgeable young man."*

Reminiscing back a pace to the first day she met Ralston on her way to her classes with a wave and a smile, and then again, shortly after her first day of school when her last class had ended, she recalled getting ready to walk alone on her way home. She hadn't gotten too far down the stairs of the middle-exit at the Department of Science and Technology Studies, before she had caught Ralston's charm out of the corner of her eye, and as he was going down the north stairs after exiting the same building and had smiled. He looked toward her, waived to her enthusiastically from a distance, and then noticed how she was struggling with the books in her hands. Without hesitation, he rushed over the lawn toward her, all too late to help her carry them. Vesha had stumbled, and her books had slipped from her grasp. Ralston then helped her pick them up, while at the same time offering her a ride home.

From that point on, Ralston J. Rayna picked Vesha up every day and became her life-long chauffeur. *"I never had to drive a car a day in my life,"* Vesha reminisced and looked at her angelic friend with a smile.

Vesha remembered the days that followed, the conversations they shared, and when they fell in love, describing her memories quietly to the angel in her mind, as if in an interview with some unseen persona, *"It must have been at some point during the many blissful, intriguing, and intellectual moments we shared. He had a depth of character I scant saw in any other man. He had an innocent charm, a love for knowledge and humanity, and he respected me through my spit, vim, and vinegar. I was in bliss in my own way, even though it was true that I was a stubborn one. I had my goals, I had shared them with Ralston, and he agreed to respect them—respect them he did,"* she recalled.

Both Vesha and Ralston attended courses under the guidance of the already renowned theoretical physicist, Dr. Philip Morrison. As with many scientists of the day, many danced close with the large budgets and goals of the US military. Dr. Morrison had been instrumental in helping with the Manhattan Project, yet after visiting the sites of the bombings of Hiroshima and Nagasaki, he founded organizations advocating the disarmament of nuclear weapons, and became a strong advocate of nuclear nonproliferation. By the time he had met Vesha and Ralston, he had changed his focus from nuclear physics to astrophysics and from there, he became well-versed in gamma-ray physics.

Vesha thought about those times, and how despite the sadness, her professor had changed his energies toward constructive pursuits.

After classes, she would find Ralston. *"Together we shared so many memories of conversations, afternoons filled with birds singing and nesting, blossoms blowing in the breeze during springtime, and leaves turning bristled colors of yellow, orange, and red through autumn. We would sip our cups of tea, only to get up scrambling, catching our papers during short gusts of wind, and chat for hours, making sense of those tenuous points in history where the stains of war seemed to result in little to show for it, other than misery and untold suffering. We would reach peace about what had happened within our minds, declare to each other that we would do what we could to never contribute to such devastation, and still get our homework done. Oh, Ralston's clarity and charm in explanation of Dr. Morrison's delivery of gamma-ray physics! I found Ralston's comprehension of each subject we discussed quite stimulating intellectually. This certainly amplified my understanding of chemistry and the Universe so much more."*

While going through their master's programs, Vesha and Ralston worked with each other, studying, and for hours on end, doing research, bouncing ideas off of each other, and it wasn't very long before they found they were growing quite a bit closer to each other. *"We would take breaks from everything at times and walk the twenty minutes it took to head northwest to Cayuga Lake, sit in the gazebo to read, and step to the shoreline to look up into the nighttime sky to see if we could spot the various constellations of the season. We would, on occasion, walk another twenty minutes to watch a play put on by the university's local comedy troupe or drama club.*

"Oh, Sky, I miss those times. Ralston was very level-headed, brilliant, enjoyed culture, and he was a gentleman with a keen sense for the arts, the sciences, and pleasantries. I felt at peace with him."

Both Vesha and Ralston had an affinity for good causes and preferred reduction in suffering and an open mind to bring an end the divisiveness throughout the world. *"We had a lot of confidence in the fact that the more we understood, the more the plight of the various cultures of humanity could be addressed. It seemed to us that at times culture, societal norms, laws that didn't protect kind and productive people but instead nitpicked the small things, and even religion if extreme toward brutality, could become an issue toward the realization of a beautiful future, especially, if we failed to step back from time-to-time and ask a few simple questions of ourselves, including the reasons why we act as we do, or do what we do. There is a micro and macro view with goals.*

"If only people could step back in life, no matter nation, creed, religion, or anything else, and engage their focus, their energies, and their efforts toward the beauty of the world we live in, if only they could focus toward the beauty of the skies, the answers laying hidden within our Universe and the Heavens, maybe misery, irrational behavior, and needless violence could be reduced." Vesha thought deeply about all of this time,

even during her young, love-filled, studious, marvelous life.

Vesha recalled, reflecting upon her past with her dream-angel, Sky, how she and Ralston had agreed that only, *"If people could be more constructive, productive, and helpful, humanity would become so much more evolved."* She knew that if we all did, *"We as people, perhaps down the road and into the future, would grow to progress toward a better reality, where we could preserve life rather than watch in shame as it was stripped away."*

Vesha knew she was surrounded by amazing people when she realized how burdened her professors had been by what had happened surrounding World War II, and the actions they took to prevent this from happening at any moment in the future.

Through Dr. Morrison's mentorship, notwithstanding his grief toward what had happened in the past, he resonated with clarity, and Vesha had begun to understand gamma-ray physics, quantum theory, and the more precise details of how large clusters of galaxies worked.

Following her first year at Cornell, Ralston asked her father, Lukas, for her hand in marriage. Ralston had told her father that they had agreed she would keep her last name, so she could carry her parents' legacy, and even help to bring in a more modern era—one of respect and of dignity. He had considered the resilience she demonstrated by doing all she needed to do, to become a scientist. Her father saw and appreciated the humanity within Ralston, was honored to consider him a son and he approved. Vesha Celeste and Ralston Rayna were married in 1948.

Throughout their lives, Ralston confided in her father how much it was that he respected her plans for a career, and he let him know that he would do all within his power to ensure that both their relationship and her career were respected.

"Family life and career goals will be seamless, respect the rigor of scientific endeavor, and complement each other," Vesha overheard Ralston telling Lukas on several occasions. Their wedding was simple, yet it was also a graceful and memorable celebration.

As they stood at the banks of Cayuga Lake, Ralston wearing his shorts, blazer, white shirt, and tie, and Vesha wearing a knee-length skirt, white blouse, and gall cross-over tie, they watched as both of their parents attended, and throughout the ceremony, they observed both of Ralston's parents and her mother and father glowing with excitement. No matter her nerves, she would look toward Ralston, and he was an endless source of stability, joy, and peace.

As time went by and they pursued their studies further, both Ralston Rayna and Vesha Celeste found that they continuously and often shared professors. "Dr. Richard Feynman took bits and pieces of ideas and notions of matter and energy in the 1940's and shaped them into the tools that ordinary physicists could understand and calculate with. He was such an honor to work with. His mannerisms made him quite a comic in his own right, making us laugh through class, while learning in a fun way and in a manner that was fulfilling," Vesha recalled.

Contemplating upon one of her other professors, she began to talk to her dream angel, Sky, again, "Dr. Hans Bethe's dedication to his work and his understanding of nucleosynthesis was extraordinary. Studying with Feynman and Bethe, sharing ideas with Ralston and working with him, my clarity of understanding grew in spades! Several of our professors became Nobel Prize winners in the '60's!"

As time went by, Vesha recalled how in 1950, she and Ralston welcomed a handsome baby boy into the world and named him Daniel. She remembered how he, at such a young age, seemed thrilled with the funny things her husband would bring home. "Ralston would bring home science books, mathematic models, and even an abacus for Daniel when he was a young child; he seemed so intrigued by how they worked. My mom and dad were involved too. They were present and helped me out regularly and faithfully. This way, Daniel had proper *parenting, while I was working on my studies and my thesis; family was a nice break from it all. Although I had to immerse myself in my studies, I still found time for him. Daniel had a loving environment."*

Vesha Celeste finished her graduate thesis in 1951, the same year her husband received his Ph.D. in chemistry. Following his graduation, Dr. Ralston J. Rayna was awarded a senior staff position at the Johns Hopkins Applied Physics Laboratory in Washington, DC.

Vesha pondered through her history, *"Ralston followed through on his promise to me, he arranged his work in DC, so I could further my education at Georgetown University for my doctoral studies. He always did the little things; he brought flowers home with a note I could see—and every bouquet looked and smelled so lovely! On so many occasions, he did things in a nuanced and quiet manner to help me out, or to make the pains of the day seem to drift away. His choices in career management enabled me to travel abroad all over the Americas, from Texas to Chile, and on to California and back, so I could gather the information necessary to write up the analysis for my thesis.*

"During my travels and studies at that time, I was able to examine the possibility of a bulk rotation in the Universe by researching the apparent expansion and how it affected or didn't affect all of the galaxies. As similar as these rotations seemed, abiding by laws of

physics, each region of space is actually unique to a fault, which adds to the complexed beauty of it all."

While at Georgetown, Vesha delivered speeches, gave seminars to professors, and pored over countless books and journals and became immersed in her studies. *"Meanwhile, Ralston juggled his private life sweetly and lovingly with me, in his professional life with brilliance, ease, responsibility, and as a father of patience and charm.*

"He became quite accomplished in his own right, and even took time for sports, engaged in community affairs and service projects, and wrote books. No matter how much was going on, he never let it slow any of us down. We also never lost our romantic spark." She loved him.

Full-bore and throughout her doctoral studies, Vesha had been paired up with many amazing professors. *"It was Ralston who had introduced me to Dr. George Gamow, who became my doctoral advisor."* She appreciated the fact that even though he was a professor working long hours at George Washington University, *"He had chosen to take time out of his schedule to spend many mind-expanding moments with me throughout my studies, providing advice and insight on nucleocosmogenesis, as I was going to Georgetown. At that time it was the only school that had a doctoral program in astronomy."* Previously, in his career, Dr.

Gamow had solved the theory of alpha decay of a nucleus via tunneling and had subsequently defected from the USSR, leading to the point in which he advised her on cosmology and quantum physics.

Vesha recalled examining the possibility of a bulk rotation in the Universe, "*In 1951, by searching for non-Hubble flow I made one of the first observations of deviations from the Hubble flow in the motions of galaxies, identifying a faster speed, a unique glow around groupings of galaxies, and a clear argument for dark matter.*"

She recalled how, while completing her thesis she had argued with Dr. Gamow, "*Galaxies might be rotating around unknown centers, rather than simply moving outwards, as suggested by the Big Bang Theory. He agreed with me shortly thereafter. However, the established scientific community saw things differently. Oh, the presentation of these ideas was not well received, and my journalistic entries were rejected by both the astronomical and the astrophysical journals, but I knew better. I needed to provide further proof, and old habits die hard. Whenever it is that skeptics seem to prevail, it is ours to search deeper and enlighten ourselves and others with concrete evidence.*"

Through it all, Vesha's parents had taught her humility so at this point in her life she realized that her data did not provide the clarity that she would have liked it to have. She knew despite all, there was something of value in her findings and argued that her thesis was significant in relation to Gérard de Vaucouleurs' claim of evidence for a "Local Supercluster."

On the home front, she gave birth to her daughter, Jillian, in 1952. As before, Vesha's parents, Lukas and Irena Celeste, eagerly helped Vesha and Ralston with their children.

Vesha recalled overhearing her parents one day talking to a reporter in an interview many years later, and Vesha had felt very much the same way about their daughter, *"We love dear sweet Jillian very much; she had been such a lovely girl, and she grew up to be interested in astronomy, just like her mother. She worked hard and earned a Ph.D. in cosmic-ray physics."*

Vesha appreciated the friend she made at the science conventions during her youth, and the earlier years of high school, as she recollected other moments shared later, *"Najem came to DC that year, in 1952, with a presentation during a science exposition that I attended. She had been working in Chicago on a study of AG Draconis and had, by a stroke of luck, discovered that its emission spectrum had completely changed since earlier observations. This was a big deal since this was one of the first observations of such a rare event documented in modern history. I also enjoyed spending time with her afterward as we talked about Andromeda and many other aspects relating to science and our personal lives for several hours."*

"It was nice rekindling our friendship after so many years of study, dedication, and she had come so far," thought Vesha.

A couple of years after her daughter Jillian's birth, Vesha completed her studies and was awarded her doctorate. Vesha reflected, *"My dissertation under Gamow, completed in 1954, made it clear that galaxies were clumped together rather than being distributed randomly throughout the Universe. This idea was not pursued by others for a couple of decades. However, I charged ahead of the pack as I dutifully completed my studies above expectations making observations well in advance of my peers. The award of Ph.D. in Astronomy was an honor."*

After receiving her doctorate, Vesha began working as a professor of mathematics and physics at the Montgomery County Community College and stayed there for a year. *"I enjoyed teaching the younger generation, and as always, there were among them some of the most brilliant people I could have ever imagined meeting. After working there for a year, I started doing what I had dreamed of doing for the longest time, which was working as a research astronomer in 1955, at Georgetown University,"* she recalled.

"*In 1956 our adorable baby boy, Chris, was born,*" Vesha reminisced with fondness. "*He later grew up to earn his doctorate in mathematics. He was a smart young man who took after his father. I could never be more proud of his dedication, his intellect, and his attentiveness to his own family when he grew up. He seemed to understand how mathematics was essential to engineering and the application of our knowledge to mechanisms that raised the quality of life.*

"*My youngest, Avery, was born in 1960 and was quite a wonderful young man as well, who loved being in the outdoors, going on hiking trips, on camping trips, and spending time near mountains, hills, lakes, rivers, and streams, even as a child. That may have been where he garnered an interest in geology. He had a theory that naturally occurring ripples in the terrain shared a calculated depth of layers related to our Earth's core layers. Manmade mountains only had dirt mixed with rock and whatever else.*

"*Brilliant,*" she chuckled quietly to herself.

She recalled carrying Avery on her hip while delivering speeches to the board, "*I gave dissertations to professors and university leaders with Avery on my hip, so someone else wouldn't provide the presentation and take sole credit for the work I had spent hours on. I juggled family life, my personal interests, and my career at the same time. They were each important to me.*"

Matthew J. Opdyke

Chapter 05: Rising in Life

Database Moon Archive, Celestial-Sol Entry Date: 2018 December 25. The following is the continuation of a brief biography, also narrated by Yesha Alevtina, and shown via a holograph presentation, where Vesha Celeste combs back into the deeper recesses of her mind despite her dementia to think back to her professional days, spending time with Najem, and meeting Jasmine, Eliza, and Yesha. This Database Moon Archive input was made by Yesha Alevtina, President of Pathway Industries, from 2015-2022.

In 1962, Vesha ran into her childhood friend, Najem, again. They took advantage of their free time and talked while they went on a hike through town to catch up on the last ten years or so of their lives.

"*It was exciting because, at this time in Najem's career, she had just accepted an administrative position at NASA. This was a first in a couple of ways—for women and for her new program, and I was very impressed. She was planning the beginning stages of travel to the Moon, involved with placing satellites in space to observe the Earth and the Universe, and two satellites, Voyager 1 and Voyager 2, were set to travel to the distant regions of our solar system. This was exciting stuff! We had to celebrate a little bit together."* Arm in arm is how she recalled spending the evening going over life, their ideas on astrophysics, and their past, and they continued later, over a couple of simple martinis.

As Vesha Celeste continued to traipse through her moments in life, she never forgot that she was always close to and appreciated her parent's religious heritage, reminiscing and remembering graciously, *"There was never a conflict for me between science and religion."*

She mused over something she was quoted as saying during an interview when a particularly vindictive reporter asked her about this apparent conflict, *"In my own life, my science and my religion are always separate. My religion suggests that I am Jewish, but religion to me is like a moral code and a sort of history. I try to do my science morally, by not developing things to hurt people, but to help people, and I believe that ideally science should be looked upon as something that helps us to understand our role in the Universe."*

Vesha reflected on her first meeting with Jasmine Belle, eleven years later. Jasmine happened to be thirty at that time, on a worker's visa from the United Kingdom in the DC area, in 1973. She was working in one of Najem's

NASA teams in preparation of several of the satellites that would be placed into outer space. *"It was an exciting time; it was a new space age, and she was brilliant!"*

Humanity's mission to the Moon, the 'space race' was on, work on the Mariner program was in full-bore, and work on the Hubble Space Telescope was filled with its challenges and ups and downs. At that same time, Vesha had been introduced by Najem to Jasmine Grace. They walked through town, but this time with Jasmine alongside them. They caught up on sciences and talked with each other more over root beer floats at the local A&W. They added Jasmine to their little circle, as they went over dark matter, astrophysics, and the future of space exploration.

Vesha then drifted, thinking about how she spent her time in the 1980s, 1990s, and 2000s. *"These decades came with some successes as well as the loss of heroes who gave their lives to science and were all-in during some of the tragedies of early pioneering space missions."* She whispered in her mind, toward her mental image of Sky hovering in the air above her, as she lay in bed.

"Oh, the people I have met; the young women, Eliza and Yesha, James, Amber and Erin, they were each an inspiration to me. Eliza and Yesha showed up to one of my conferences instead of going to their prom, in 1994, and that is some original thought, spunk, and tenacity. I

admire those girls. Our subsequent discussions and meetings from time to time over the last almost two decades were always so vibrant, full of life, meaning, and intellectuality. I remember talking with them about the usual, and Eliza seemed especially intrigued. Hah, those two sweet young ladies, they certainly have great potential. They burn from within to do great things. I am pleased with Eliza, proud of her for finally running for office, with a successful bid at that, to represent her state in the United States Congress. I am also proud of Yesha, for the support and wisdom she has shown through the years too. It can be difficult to muddle through life alone, but it's worse getting by feeling lonely. I've been alone for a few years, but they've had each other's back since day one."

Vesha reflected on the meetings with the Pathway science teams. *"What a time for science, although it was a covert set of operations, Eliza and Yesha and James, Amber, and Erin, wow! They have done so much in the last eight years with little praise to show for it. So many lives have been blessed because of their care and their efforts."* Sky was smiling quietly, proud of Vesha.

Vesha also recalled when she spent time with Najem and Jasmine in the new Pathway facilities. Her encounters with young Amber, James, and little Erin were all so sweet and endearing. She thought of all that had passed through her gaze in life despite her advancing years and the contributions she had made, the many brilliant people who had brought her in—if for anything out of admiration of her efforts in science and her love for humanity.

She admired both Eliza and Yesha, as they grew to be very competent scientists, adults, and leaders, multiplying their ingenuity and compounding upon it at every turn. She applauded them for their self-motivation to improve things in the world and to make the core of well-being and quality of life the driving force for what they did. She also reflected on how she had spent a long life serving her world and humanity in her own way, in the search for wisdom, knowledge, and understanding of space and all of its exhilarating intrigues.

She had written many scientific journal entries for the public audience, had made amazing discoveries that pushed physics into the palpable, with astronomical, quantum, and particle physics subjects and a more profound grasp of dark matter and the cosmic microwave background (CMB) both in public and private.

Early on, in 2000 is when she had begun to show signs of an increase of dementia, however, she did everything she could to delay its effects. *"Perhaps that's why Eliza and Yesha pleaded with me to join Pathway. They knew I wanted to live a natural life, they respected that, and they are allowing me to make a different decision in my own time. I can't recall all of the details of what we did together, but I do know we met a lot of wonderful people who at one point were struggling and living in environments I would not wish on my worst enemy, and they too stepped up to the plate and helped so many more."*

Together with her late and beloved husband, Ralston, she had taught, mentored, and loved her children until they too had expressed their own doctoral expertise. Ralston had been an incredible tennis player, a mathematician, and a physicist in his own right, and had passed away at the age of eighty-one. *"Oh, how I miss him, and I'll never forget how heavy it was for me when he closed his eyes for the last time,"* she thought, with a tear running down her right cheek and a smile which was evidence of how proud of him she was and how much she loved him.

Vesha had provided instruction to countless fellows and many more students; she had been honored by the Washington Academy of Sciences, and together with Ralston she had taught their grandchildren about the many wonders of the Universe. *"Your grandmother was an astronomer, because the stars and the grand cosmos was always something that she loved deeply and cared so much about, and there is always so much to learn and appreciate about our Universe,"* Vesha thought, almost in a quiet conversation to her future generations. With dementia settling in, she did what she could to retain her memories, even if it required a conversation with her dream angel, Sky, who was hovering above her bed in an understanding posture with the mural of Andromeda behind her glowing back, resting on the ceiling above.

Generations of family Vesha would soon be leaving behind had visited that day, those she had missed would soon be standing before her, and her visitors left her there in pleasant solitude contemplating the time she spent with them and how she would soon be leaving them for the next great journey of the unknown. She hadn't thought of her dream angel for decades, until those years when her dementia seemed ready to abscond with another memory or two. *"Sky, you visited me when I needed you most. Lately, you have visited me even more. You reminded me that together we could succeed in life, that our dreams and goals are precious, with you and Ralston we successfully balanced our family and personal lives, even our magnificent careers, and while whispers of the Nobel Peace Prize were just that, whispers, we ought to be pleased with the notion of simply having helped people out."*

She looked up as her eyes adjusted to the darkness assisted by the dim flicker of the night light and slightly smiled as she faintly made out the seemingly glowing mural of Andromeda on her ceiling above. She closed her eyes to sleep that eternal sleep, as the tug of the Universe began to take its effect, to beckon, to call for her, as she gave way to this riptide of life, she let go allowing the waves to take her away. It was as if Sky was there with her all along, to help her on her next big journey, smiling, speaking to her mind the words of comfort, care, dignity, and love.

With knowledge solely of a beginning and an end to every turn and twist of fate, Vesha would soon become one with her Universe again, her memories, her particles, and her dreams would now be a part of that vital substance that would usher in new life, and perhaps a different life ripe with her own cognizance in the future.

Chapter 06: Arpeggios of Harmony

Database Moon Archive, Celestial-Sol Entry Date: 2018 December 25. The following is the continuation of Vesha Celeste's experiences and the beginning of a whole new way of seeing life, in a manner she had never thought possible before. This Database Moon Archive input was made by Yesha Alevtina, President of Pathway Industries, from 2015-2022.

After Vesha sighed, she felt at peace, and after closing her eyes, she blissfully lost herself in her dreams flying away with Sky on journeys of daring-do, of honor, of love, and shared understanding between one civilization or another, and then she began to feel young and vibrant, and with a unique and sudden clarity of mind. Vesha realized she could hear just as clearly as when she was ten; she no longer felt the need for sleep. Something was different about her surroundings, but she couldn't quite place what it was or where she was. Instead, Vesha started to enjoy everything she had contemplated as beautiful as if it were music that was playing in the air around her. *"Where am I?"*

She decided to lie there for a while. Vesha felt young again, and she imagined the sounds of arpeggios as if they were finely tuned pianos playing away harmoniously, a symphony of waves, the chiming of clocks, and the knocking of the door that had hummed synchronously as if a beautiful tune were permeating throughout her entire living space.

The door knocked again, as if to create a sense that grounded her and helped her to perceive a new reality.

The music seemed that it had quieted to lower decibels; her blissful errands seem to fade from reality, and her friendly and lovely dream angel began to disappear from before her, but somehow, she did so with an understanding farewell, the look of the wise, and a wave of her hand, and then she smiled before looking down and fading completely. It seemed as if the music were still playing within the background of her mind, but it too had begun to fade just as fast. And then Vesha realized that she had indeed heard another "tap" at the actual door.

"Oh my," she thought, as she slowly came to, from what seemed a deep slumber. *"I must be losing my mind. Do I have a visitor?"*

As soon as Vesha realized someone was at the door, she sprang from her covers like she did when she was in her youth, unaware that things had changed. There was a slight glow emanating from her skin, but she did not notice luminescent sparkles as she rushed to flick the light on. When it seemed to be the switch was in a different location, she stopped. *"That's odd."* She thought.

She saw her mural of Andromeda still on the ceiling above, her eyes had adjusted to the darkness, more quickly than she was used to, and then she saw her Van Gogh of "A Starry Night" on the wall near the doorway, but something was wildly different about the environment she was in and there was the switch.

"There is something up with and unusual about this," Vesha mumbled in her mind, and dismissed it as she gathered herself together, not wanting to keep her visitor waiting. She managed to find and place her fluffy warm slippers over the socks on her feet, and then recovered and wrapped her robe around her black and silky nightgown feeling a vibrancy she hadn't felt in decades. A tingling sensation reverberated throughout her body as if her skin were radiating a beautiful light accompanied by a more intense euphoria on her left side. Upon finding the light switch, she turned it on and headed toward the door.

"Vesha," she could hear a gentle and beautifully recognizable voice, followed by a softer tap at the door, and then a pause. The visitor was ever-so-patient and persistent.

Vesha called back through the hallway door toward the plausible entrance, from whence came the knocking, and noticed a younger timber to her own voice as she, in a kind and urgent manner, responded, "I'm coming! Sorry to make you wait. I seem to be a little confused, but I am on my way, and I'll be there in just a second!" After uttering those words, she knew something was indeed different about her own situation, and she could not yet figure out what it could be.

Vesha arrived at the door, looking into the security display above it of a video image of her visitor. On the other side of the entryway was an angelic face beset with a familiar, peaceful, and serene smile. On the porch was a most interesting, feminine, and exquisitely framed and beautifully dressed, nicely busted young lady, with medium-length hair in an up-do, a rainbow of highlights through her professionally groomed brunette locks. It donned on her that on the other side of the barrier was a recognizable young lady, and with no desire to keep her waiting any longer, she opened the door and greeted her lovely visitor.

"I'm Yesha Alevtina," said this entrancing, somewhat familiar emerald and hazel-eyed, beautiful brunette, who appeared to be a petite young lady, and with a mind-catching intellectual delivery of her speech.

As she spoke, her words twisted like ageless and confectionery perfection in the air through her perfect and pouty lips. "I hope you recognize me? How are you doing? You're Vesha Celeste, correct? We met more than twenty years ago for the first time, and you visited us as an honorary member of Pathway several times. May I come in? There is so much to do, and we have a lot to discuss."

"Of course," said Vesha Celeste, making motions to enter her dwelling and wondering what there was so to do, and what it was they were going to chat about. At first, she thought that her dementia was confusing her perception of reality, but she let that concern dissipate as she opened the screen door further to politely let her come in. Yesha gently brushed by her, giving Vesha a gentle sensation as if life outside of her own had made contact and provided her a living reference point beyond her own mind. Directing Yesha to a comfortable couch, certain aspects of her reality and the setting she was in came to her all of a sudden. Her living facility resembled more of a home, the furniture was white and smooth and soft, and aside from other essential aspects of her main living quarters, things had changed rather drastically. She wasn't in a senior citizen's center anymore, that much was apparent; she was in an actual home, or so it seemed. Yesha was right, there might be a few things to do and a discussion beforehand might help—she was confused.

Vesha looked down and noticed that although her hands were slightly balmy and shivering, they were also glimmering and young. Gone were the wrinkles on the surfaces of the dermis visible to her, gone were the places where too much sun had kissed her skin for too long or too often, and before her, her hands and wrists were smooth, of pleasant scent, and silky—cleared away were the marks of age. She felt an unusual tingling sensation on her left shoulder, the left of her chest, breast, and on her left arm and down past her left hip, thigh, and down to her foot, and despite all, she ignored it.

She offered this dazzling beauty sitting on the couch before her some naturally sweetened and warmed herbal hydration—a favorite of hers—a dried hibiscus from Asia.

In a soft yet assertive, attractive, yet serenely excited voice, Yesha accepted, "Of course. I love the wonderful varieties of tea, and Asian hibiscus is among my favorites. They have so many natural and good qualities for our bodies. It's a shame that herbal teas are all-too-often overlooked and under-appreciated in many places throughout the world. Thank you, Vesha," and Yesha smiled as she sipped her tea.

"I've felt the same way for years as well," agreed Vesha.

After a few moments of quiet retreat, Yesha smiled with appreciation toward her pleasant agreement and continued, "I am so glad to see you. You can't imagine my excitement. First of all, it's been a while. I am curious, how do you feel? Do you know where you are? Have you seen yourself, yet? Because sitting here with you right now, you look amazing. Please humor me? We've sipped some tea, so could you please head past your kitchen, and then head just one room further than your bedroom to your bathroom on the right? Once you do, can you please take a look at yourself in the mirror? When you do, please tell me what you think?"

While Vesha appreciated the compliment, questions about where she thought she was and if she had seen herself in the mirror, seemed quite unique. There was no ridicule or sarcasm in her voice, yet she knew something was up. Vesha was pretty sure she was in a senior citizen's living facility, within her own domicile, and with her private balcony, at least that's where she had been earlier. Or so it seemed. Vesha hadn't looked at herself since the previous morning. She hadn't showered since the day before, or before the seasonal celebrations, and she still thought of herself as a finely-aged eighty-eight-year-old lady. Despite Yesha's sincere tone, she couldn't help but think that maybe she was just trying to be polite. Perhaps Yesha was pointing out that she was in all reality merely a mess. Vesha calmly rushed to the restroom to check. When she looked into the mirror, she couldn't believe what she beheld.

"Oh, my...!" Vesha exclaimed standing in her pajamas and robe, so used to the expressions and mannerisms of someone who had lived the eighty-eight years she had. The young person on the other side of the mirror gazed at her in disbelief. She liked what she saw; it reminded her of an amazingly artistic and spectacularly youthful, curvy, slender, and perky version of distant memories of something resembling herself. However, on this particular occasion for as much as she tried, she only distantly remembered each of her youthful features from so long ago. It was rare to consider, but Vesha was, in fact, beholding a reflection from her twenty-two-year-old days.

Chapter 07: Acceptance

Database Moon Archive, Celestial-Sol Entry Date: 2018 December 25. The following is the continuation of Vesha Celeste's experiences and her beginning of a whole new way of life, and in a state, she had never thought possible before. This Database Moon Archive input was made by Yesha Alevtina, President of Pathway Industries, from 2015-2022.

Yesha smiled as she sensed Vesha's excitement and well-given wonder and felt giddy inside for the first time in a long while, relatively speaking.

"I look... different! What exactly happened? Wait, you asked where I thought I was, and now I am at a loss; what is this place, and where am I?" Vesha had a thousand questions as she stood in baffled amazement, not used to her youthful yet wise and assertive voice, looking at the state-of-the-art technology in the bathroom. It hadn't sunk in that her environment had a glowing white aura, the sinks were spacious, and every item in the bathroom was as if it were one gigantic and carved out piece of glowing white marble, yet with sophisticated technology imbued into it, with every imaginable update provided, and all of it through-the-roof-awesome!

After taking in that bit of reality, she found herself momentarily at a state of disbelief at what she beheld looking back at her from the mirror. Instead of working herself into a baffled frenzy, she found herself even more excited by her newly perceived reality. Enchanted and in awe, she thought out loud, loud enough for Yesha to hear. "I won't lie, Yesha, I thought there was something odd about my living quarters, and I believed I was dying about twenty minutes ago. This bathroom is amazing, and this young lady on the other side of the mirror is beautiful!

"Putting the pieces together, I had some pretty deep and fleeting moments of memory as if my life were playing before my eyes, and a bit of a headache.

"Afterward, I started heading off into dreamland.

"The second I sighed, breathed out, and thought I wouldn't breathe in again, it was then and quite precisely when my pain was gone, I felt vibrant and like I could reach the stars! Yesha, it's starting to become clear now, and no, you're not just a familiar visitor, you're a long-time friend!" Her neural nanos were working hard and she saw herself glow as her physiology and neurology were connecting all the sectors of cells and neurons in an optimal way, "But, I must have died, and you brought me back. How many years went by?"

Against every prudent aspect of the nature of personal expression that she was used to—one of humility and calm reserve, she began to ogle her reflection in the mirror divested of shame or narcissism, but filled with excitement and wonder, "Wow! I think I might actually like this! It dons on me now with quickened clarity that for years I was a bit more, how should I put it? I was too prudent during the last few decades of my life! However, to my credit, I was lost in noble pursuits, not to mention I'd been suffering from dementia. Oh my, I wonder what my friends and family would think if they saw me now. What about my surviving children, Daniel, Chris, Avery, and their and Jillian's families, what would they think? How would they react?"

A subtle yet fleeting moment of terror passed through her as she thought about their reactions. Perhaps feelings of anger would surface and maybe even a sense of jealousy would boil through their blood, fester with their minds, and flow to freedom through their actions, but then her mind grew clear, and she realized how her family had always been kind and understanding.

The more her neural nanos created additional healthy links in her mind, the more Vesha realized how wonderful this entire experience was. It was clearer to her now, she had raised her children to respect noble pursuits, to love life, and appreciate the splendor of shared time. Vesha then thought how anyone of a healthy mind would be overjoyed and gracious, especially if they had been given this set of circumstances.

As more memories of her mortal life surfaced, she found herself thinking out loud, "I loved my family then, and I still do now. Nevertheless, I suppose this is my life and my reality now to choose whatever whim and detail I wish with reckless abandon and with no more doubt of self-expression; there's much ahead. Wow, Yesha!"

With an immediate sense of guilt that hung over from Vesha's previous life and her commitment to her values and doubts, it was as if pulsating waves of thoughts about her parents, her husband, and children had crept in and her concern arose again. This time she was worried that she was merely justifying her current reality, simply because she was happy with it. It took Vesha a moment to find a sense of clarity with this new wave of thoughts.

The constraints she put on herself were hers alone to deal with. They were not sourced in from any other direction. As the neural nanos cleared the areas of her mind that were capable of taking an outside view of experiential relativity, as if it were a game on the field, she shook it off, "I abided by the values my parents espoused throughout my life and I still appreciate everything I was taught, learned, and subsequently shared with my children. They grew up to be wonderful people. They were individuals who I still respect and love, no matter how they expressed themselves. It's now my turn to live and be free to express myself how I desire, and to be loved while living free and by my own whims," she voiced out loud.

As Vesha coached herself, she felt the freedom of her new reality sweep in and then she rejected her concerns and worries, because they were her very own critical views of herself, ones she had deemed the judgments of others, but they instead were perceptions she had of yesteryear, "Now is a new day. I have slept for some time, and I have no memories whatsoever of that timeless slumber. I can remember my life as clear as day now, before this moment that I am currently experiencing, and I can see who I am. I mean, I can't help it, look at me, there she is before me. My inner and outer beauty are connected and sharing the same message!

"Here I am now, and though I thought I had died, I'm quite alive, and, Wow! I feel more alive than ever, with potential oozing from every pore. My reflection tells me I'm ravishing! I can't stop looking, I'm so amazed! Who am I? Wait, I'm myself, but younger, yet with all of my memories coming in as if they were yesterday, or a few minutes ago! What's the breadth of the changes? What can I do? What are my limits?"

"Fancy you asked," said Yesha, smiling and proud of Vesha's first responses. Yesha understood Vesha's reactions, because she had been in her shoes, at least to a certain degree before. Although she had never actually died, she remembered how it felt as every cell quivered into some sort of euphoria before releasing her inner will and finding the immensity of joy that comes with an optimized body and mind. On the day that she and Eliza had used the biopods for the first time, she too had had her mind racing with questions she never thought to ask before, and then like that, a surge of answers streamed in moments later with complete clarity. Fortunately, she was not alone in that experience, because both she and Eliza had pioneered the first biopod trial ever, and together.

Yesha was pleased with all aspects of Vesha's reactions to everything she beheld and felt.

Vesha showed depth in character, even signs that she indeed was the woman Yesha had grown to admire for more than two decades. She admired the fact that Vesha was embracing her new and wondrous reality so quickly.

Bringing Vesha Celeste back from the dead required a lot of science, a lot of care, and a lot of hard work, and as a result, Yesha Alevtina was glad that her heavy involvement in the full spectrum of results was reciprocated through Vesha's excitement.

"You are still the amazing you that you always were, Vesha. You are now a magnified and miraculous result of a collaborative effort of science, of love, and of dedication. You are a twenty-two-year-old version of you, with some extra, pleasant, and optimum aspects to your entire range of abilities and aesthetic, your physiology, and your physical and neural capacities.

"In theory, your limits are few, but your nature is benevolent to the core. I've seen you, known you, and appreciate everything about you. Since you are innately capable of benevolent actions and virtuous internal character, your abilities will multiply with little chance of losing them. Someone would practically have to hurl you into the Sun to harm you to any effect, and I'm sure you might even be able to endure that and come out okay.

"Vesha, you are remarkable in every way, you have tremendous and nearly unlimited potential, and what you choose to do with it lies within you alone.

"You will be able to learn anything, absorb so much more than before, pretty much everything you wish, travel anywhere, and do anything you put your mind to. My sweet friend, you will have the capacity to resolve some of the most rigorous issues known to mankind both in this world and throughout the Universe."

Vesha continued to look into the mirror and beheld herself with awe and a hearty side-dish of disbelief, but despite all, she beheld what she saw with an internal and increasing excitement, filled with gratitude.

"I suppose this is where it all starts. It all starts within each of us and goes out from there. What do you think of the tattoos and rainbow highlights in your hair?"

"I am impressed with your work, Yesha. This is unimaginable, yet so lovely! Who would have thought of this arrangement? Who would have guessed I would have been so amused? I am blown away by the aqua, the turquoise, the green, the rich purple, and the soft yellow highlights. I suppose I might never have imagined this in such a way, so many beautiful variations and shades that truly do complement my curly brunette angle-bobbed hair."

"Your right brain and its inventive processes are responsible for your look, and you are very creative," Yesha explained. "Look at the tattoo-like artwork on your left side, as it swirls and moves around. We didn't hire any artists for the intricate artwork, if we had, they would have made a viable fortune, it is your mind doing this.

"What do you think?"

Vesha thought about the question quickly and responded, "I'm still so amazed at my hair and my skin. I haven't seen anything resembling this face on myself in the mirror in decades, who would have thought that these extra details could bring so much wonder? The eye-catching colors—the locks of hair, I like how they match my eyes and everything else! I understand what you're saying about the regional and right-brain-controlled outward expressions of what I look like, in some cases my eyes, hair, and makeup seem to adjust every moment, like a large ship on a series of ocean waves, modifying smoothly and unnoticeably.

"I presume it was you and Eliza, who made most of this possible? If so, you guys did a wonderful job! I always knew you two had genius minds. I am impressed. Thank you to both of you!" In an excited sense of inquisitiveness, Vesha asked, "Is there a brief explanation as to how all of this was possible? You asked about the tattoo-like artwork!? Oh, I haven't checked! Okay, sorry. I will look. Let's see."

Vesha paused as she untied and dropped her silk garments and beheld the fullness of splendor of her new physical and youthful attributes.

"Whatever it is that I had been feeling earlier—that tingling sensation on my left side when I got up to answer the door, it must be related to those, to these?" She paused again and began to realize that just as her body adjusted to its new system, as if in a complexed and harmonious symphony, something was optimizing and changing her internally impacting and adjusting her external artwork at every moment. The magnificence of it all hit her for a moment with inaudible gratitude. As the artwork adjusted, it was as if it were a series of scenes from a silent movie, and instead of causing pain, these changes filled her with euphoria and vibrancy. Vesha then glowed as she healed or adjusted.

"If that is the case now, if I am glowing because of the upgrades and adjustments now, the same could be true when my body is optimizing no matter where I might be, in private or public." It hit her, she might want to be discreet when in public and learn how to control it.

"Not only do the colors of my tattoo-like artistry intensify, but each shape and the intricate details on my physique change in form, almost continuously, like a picture-screen with sophisticated imagery in motion throughout various areas of my body, while leaving my skin aglow as I heal and upgrade."

In the bathroom, after she had shed her wardrobe to see the changes, Vesha graciously continued to talk to Yesha about her artwork, "Yesha? Wow! I haven't pictured myself like this in years! I was in the world for eighty-eight good ones, and aging took its toll, sagging, greying, and wrinkling, and I accepted its prettiness in my own way. Oh, I earned every bit of the wear and tear, but I would never have even imagined this was possible! Oh, wow, Yesha! My mind is blown!

"I remember when you told us about optimized physiology before I passed away, and I said I would live life out naturally. I arranged it so after my funeral, I would donate what was left to Pathway, for science. Knowing me, I am pretty sure that I wouldn't have approved of any of this, or its peculiarity. In a way, I suppose I was willing, since I donated my body for research with at least a little inkling of hope in you guys.

"I always believed, before seeing what I am seeing now, that aging in grace was gorgeousness in its own right; letting nature take its course was the moniker for dealing with senescence and death in the past. Death was a part of Nature's evolution with so many mixed results, but here I am, alive as can be, and with every result as desirable as my imagination allows it to be.

"My body was an empty tapestry just waiting for a masterpiece of self-expression before I passed away, and I took an almost quiet and condescending tone of minor judgment against those wearing artistry, but here I am, and here is the art, ornate, exquisite, and so expressive, and I like it. My apologies to all for not appreciating others as much as I ought to have for their self-expression before. This skin art is a part of me! Seeing what I see, knowing what I know, and feeling what I feel? It's magnificent!

"Wow, I can see my dream angel, Sky, moving around within my body-murals! Sky was such a lovely friend to me, during the worst of it all! I can tell you with full confidence that I approve of this and its oddities more than one-hundred percent, if that's possible, Yesha!"

Vesha was awash in enthusiasm and excitement. Deep down, she was thrilled and extremely impressed with the turn of events, courtesy of her friends. Vesha knew that it wasn't vanity to appreciate the merging of natural and humanity-driven evolution. The proof stood before her in the mirror and existed within the increasing clarity of her mind. She contemplated how, with speed, all she had ever learned and felt was multiplying in her mind and her body in both complexity and meaning. It became as clear as day to Vesha that she was now, everything she could have ever imagined being, feeling, and hoping for.

Vesha looked upon her renewed physical facial features, her pouty, full, and perfect lips, her slightly upturned nose and its soft point and was trying not to be smitten with herself. She couldn't help it though. Her smoothly-chiseled chin and high cheeks, her hair that was full in volume and color again, and her eyebrows perfectly trimmed without the need for effort, were any woman's dream. She gathered the courage to look upon her naked body, and with awe and disbelief, she could not take her eyes away from her newfound youth, her perfection, and all of its splendor—her tight skin, her firm yet soft curves, her colors, and her perky faultlessness.

"I normally would not have found it within me to look at myself like this, or even ask, but I will now. What do you think, Yesha? Please look, I trust you; this is amazing! You've performed a scientific miracle!

"Thank you, Yesha!

"How did you and Eliza do it?"

Yesha walked into the hallway from the living room and stood to the left of the bathroom entrance, with her back against one wall gazing across the hall opposite the doorway—mostly to maintain Vesha's sense of privacy for now, until she was sure Vesha was just a little more comfortable in her new skin.

Yesha then responded to Vesha's question, "It wasn't easy, we had your DNA, your full-on genetic code, and your entire neural network. It was recorded within our Twelve Database Moons, courtesy of the preservation transceivers placed into your system when you became an honorary member of Pathway, and then the notification alerted us from the app on your smartphone, that you had passed away. Luckily, the neural link between your mind and smartphone beamed everything we needed to the Twelve Database Moons and recorded everything about you, down to your last thoughts, before your final breath.

"Everything we needed to bring you back was available to work with, and it is clear now that we achieved as close to perfection as possible while retaining your will, your memories, your 'you-ness,' and here you are.

"So, yes, Vesha Celeste, you are still the amazing 'You' that you ever were and always have been; only now, your physiology has been optimized to near perfection in every possible and conceivable way. As you may have noticed, many will have difficulty not appreciating how beautiful you are, because your mind shows your inner and outer beauty.

"As you already noted, your artistic right-brain definitely has a say in your appearance to a certain degree, given all that was done—the hair, the colors, and the artwork. Seeing life pulsate through you again certainly brings my heart some peace and joy.

"Vesha, it indeed took a lot of work, a lot of study time, and again, even more work, but at last we did it. Eliza, James, Amber, Erin, Najem, Jasmine, and many of your friends at Pathway were involved. Despite all, I am so glad you approve. I'm impressed with you and your progress in such a short period of time!

"There is a lot about you that we updated in order to optimize your physiology and neurology, so I am sure you are aware we'll need to familiarize and train you on all of your upgrades, as well as show you what you can do. Eventually, you will learn how to 'normalize' the glow and the root of it. Your right brain will soon be able to take control of what you allow others to see of you more fully.

"Right now, we can't run around in public, either, while you're looking like a glow-in-the-dark person of the future. I mean, I can glow like you are if I choose, but, since your body and mind are making adjustments and enhancements and you are kind of going through a state of shock and glowing in a lesser controlled fashion, it is better that we wait. You'll have an opportunity to head out into the real world after training.

"Throughout our mentoring process there, we'll help you to learn to adjust your age as needed. Right now, you look like you did when you were twenty-two, with some extra aesthetic miracles of expression. If you'd like, you can adapt your age anytime to look anywhere between twenty and thirty-five years without looking too obviously out of the norm. There's no problem with personal expression or age, per say, we just need to be dialed down in our artistic appearance, when it comes to creative display, so we don't stand out in an obvious way. Looking youthful is a great idea, because fewer people will notice any oddities, especially since there is a great quantity of our youthful population that can be quite creative in their expressions anyway.

"Nonetheless, we will help you to learn how to create compartmentalized wardrobes and personalized facial and body imagery in your mind to avoid too much suspicion from anyone, outside of Pathway. Your unique facial construct and physique will always be you as if you were in the ideal condition, but certain aspects of artwork and imagery will still be yours to manipulate and hold in place. Right now, as you may have noticed, I've allowed my hair to express itself artistically, because we are at the Pathway Campus in Melrose, Massachusetts.

"I convey a conservative or professional vibe for my visual appearance in public, but from time to time, situation depending, I will let loose.

"In the coming years, we will all be able to allow ourselves to let go a little more in public, to be as creative as we wish to be, but only marginally. Once Eliza has convinced the Senate, and the associated powers-that-be, to allow physiological and neurological reanimation and optimization as an option, humanity will have all of this available to them based on personal choice and consent.

"It's still an uphill battle right now, however, and for far too many reasons to explain at the moment. While somewhat frustrating, only in the purview of anyone of a sound mind would it seem that arguing against having optimized physiology and neurology is a sad way to expend one's energy. Seriously, doesn't it seem a waste of time on their part to discourage something so wonderful? I do believe that if chaos is their personal choice, so long as it doesn't hurt anyone, I can respect that.

"What do you think?"

Vesha understood the social dilemmas of so much progress so fast, and for a moment she got lost in thought. *"The perspectives of society are indeed limiting when it comes to personal expression and the sharing of each aspect of our attractiveness, whether internal or external. Although new to my present reality, I know that nothing expressed by anyone in Pathway suggests brutality or grotesqueness; still, people are unnerved by something that they don't understand, and it is unfortunate for so many, in the least helpful of ways.*

"There were many in my day that didn't let half the population become scientists; something as simple as that was considered taboo.

"Society could do so much more, though, if they didn't make rules that had nothing to do with the well-

being of others. Instead, they seem to discourage things like this for all that they are worth.

"Society and governance would be better off if they didn't arbitrarily make rules, laws, and muddy the waters of ethics in ways that aren't very ethical, while making enemies of others, engaging in witch-hunts and generalizing vast swaths of people—of innocent, unique, and beautiful people."

Vesha knew that as a whole, society would be better off if they could focus on healing, optimizing, and preserving life. Vesha felt that doing so would lead to a beautiful reality. After contemplating for a brief moment, she thought about her friend, Eliza.

Without realizing she was doing so, for the first time Vesha had activated her neurological link and communicated to everyone who had been trained and optimized within Pathway, and then she did it again, thinking she was quietly whispering within her own mind.

"Thank you again, Eliza and Yesha, my friends, and thank you to all of our friends at Pathway. Each of you did an excellent job and this life standing before me right here is indeed a labor of love. This is amazing!

Vesha continued, but this time out loud, "So, Eliza, is in the Senate now. I am so happy she is there. I always knew she had a gift for leadership and decisions! I have no doubt she is winning over close colleagues, rubbing shoulders with the right leaders, and influencing people where it seems the big decisions are made. I wouldn't mind visiting her at work to see how they keep our country functioning, sometime soon, if that is okay? She was always an inspiration. I am proud of her. No doubt she's had some political battles along the way.

"Doing the guesswork, I presume it has been at least two years since I passed away?" asked Vesha.

"You are correct, Vesha. It has been two years."

Vesha then thought about how her physiology would work, if she were to meet someone, special. "So, I have a question." Vesha paused, "How does my body, um, work? I mean, if I do meet a wonderful person, will I be able to have family down the road, or maybe choose to hold off while on distant journeys to the great unknown throughout and beyond our massive Universe, while still having the splendor of a relationship with someone?"

Relieved she had asked this, Yesha explained. "This has been such a hot-button issue in society, and we have done everything we can within the development of our technologic advances to afford women their own choice when it comes to their bodies while avoiding issues that could potentially countermand the beliefs of those who might be religious regarding having children."

Yesha had known why her team considered this for some time and continued to answer her inquisitive friend, "If you are ever in that special moment with someone, all you have to do is ask, are you ready for a family? Yes or no? If they aren't ready, or you're not ready, then enjoy that special moment. As a matter of fact, if someone is not ready, then the conception will never occur, and no matter the choice, the nanos in your body will add extra health, as well as glowing and colorful light, delightful sensations, and phenomenal pleasure. If you are ready, then you will have the option of childbirth in less than a week, and your child will receive all of the nurture he or she will need to grow into an amazing, healthy, brilliant, and loving individual in a matter of weeks. They will become mature as soon as necessary with the Health and Education Matrices, available in the Virtual Universe, or a person can choose to rear their children organically."

"That's amazing, Yesha. What a weighty ordeal that has been for years! It has been lifted and enmity gone. Who would have known? This is a delightful day!"

Yesha smiled, "Yes, that ordeal has been resolved and those fears and worries are no longer necessary. Now, there is little need for people to feel compelled to go through with bringing more children into the world if they are not ready or if the resources surrounding them are meager at best. In the reverse, if they are at a time in their lives they deem appropriate or right for that significant responsibility, they can go ahead with hope and joy.

"We have always sensed that people should not be deprived of intimacy and that it is a shared responsibility between two persons to enjoy their connections with each other, in a manner of consent. People should allow their inner love and desire for happiness, together, blossom in so many ways.

"We've always loved children, so it is nice to know that once they are born, at least in Pathway and the many Pathway tech cities, each child will be brought into an environment where they are loved, nurtured, and given everything needed to be successful within their own lives.

"Women, as a result, will have an opportunity to decide on whether or not this is a good time to have families from the very beginning, without fear, death, or controversy. Instead, their decisions will be made with love and the ability to provide the desired result, while still allowing them to be beholden to their faith if that is what drives them to be the wonderful people they are. Eliza has always promoted diversity."

"I don't believe it is possible to answer that question any more eloquently. You did good Yesha."

Realizing that Yesha was waiting outside the bathroom, she called her in and opened the door a little wider in order to allow Yesha the opportunity to appreciate her work, "Yesha, please come in, no worries."

Yesha turned to see Vesha and explained who had aided in her development and subsequent awakening, "Vesha, a lot has changed since you've passed away, as far as life is concerned. I must be fair, as far as your return to the world of the living is concerned, it wasn't just Eliza and me who helped to bring you back. Amber Blythe, Erin Carter, Najem Grace, and Jasmine Belle were in on much of this as well. Even James Cooper helped."

Yesha saw Vesha's right eyebrow raise into a peak, and trying not to laugh, knowing she was receptive to humor, she continued, "No worries; James helped with certain aspects of the scaffolding of your various organs and your skeletal structure.

"He took his panache for construction and multiplied it in spades to learn various other sciences, to include biotechnology, data processing, and neuroscience using the training capacities in the Virtual Universe.

"Besides, if he did see you, he was very respectful and dignified. The people in Pathway have an innocent mindset about all of that. Vesha, we had quite a team working with us." said Yesha, and then she examined the perfection of her dear old friend's new look—she was impressed with the results, and the fact that Vesha was now very much alive again, and remarkably so. Yesha almost cried tears of joy seeing that Vesha was awake and aware and no longer laying lifeless in Pathway's labs.

Yesha continued, "Your body's artistry and your hair are all related and synced to your neural network and activity. As we have talked about, your right brain has now unleashed in certain harmless ways a beautiful set of expressions, kind of like a spiraling-kaleidoscope set of mandala patterns, galaxies, stars, flowers, an angel, and so much more. Your right brain, she certainly gets a say!

"It appears that Sky is quite deep with symbolism and artistic expression. I must note, I like how your mind's artistry wraps that beautifully frosted mandala pattern around your area, right there," Yesha pointed, but did not touch her, "And it dissipates in just the right places. It's something else, the beauty of the mind. Physically, every aspect of you is angelic and extremely gorgeous," Yesha said emotionally, with fascination for the beauty of life.

"You mentioned Sky? I suppose when my last thoughts were uploaded, perhaps you saw her?" Vesha was not sure at first whether to be embarrassed about this new revelation regarding her dream angel or not, but somehow Yesha had mentioned her, so she asked.

"I know about Sky. She is beautiful, with hair the color of icicles, with iridescent highlights throughout. There is nothing to be embarrassed about, Vesha. She is magnificent in every way. Please note, that from a view based in established science, different and significant regions of the brain identify themselves in diverse ways and at different times. Your right mind appears to express herself as a lovely, powerful, and very creative angel with nearly glowing white blonde hair, a rainbow of highlights, and soft pink and supple lips. Although she looks different than you do, Sky is definitely having a big say on what you look like. Both of you look and are beautiful!

"Although you are a composite of your left and right mind, as well as your prefrontal cortex, among other regions of your awareness, your 'you-ness' is actually a summation of all that you are, linked via your corpus callosum, and as such, standing before me as we speak. It was mostly and purely by accident that we discovered these new artistic features and loved them, and with all that we know, there is something very special about her.

"Given all of the rest of the benefits of indefinite lifespans, reawakening you from the dead, and optimized physiology and neurology, we brought you back as human as we could. Throughout your life, you both had a special connection. The additions you have to your gifted abilities include so much, but healing, resistance, strength, and survivability capabilities, even beyond our own is just the beginning of it all, and Sky was a part of that.

"We were very much pleased with the results, and I'm glad you are. In Pathway, those of us who have been fully read-in, we each have significant upgrades and the ability to do many of the things you do now. But Vesha, you are superior, you are unique, and you are currently the only one as powerful as you are, which I presume is all due to your alter ego, named Sky. Throughout your life, you harbored no aggression toward anyone and always demonstrated intrigue in the truths of our Universe as well as a desire for the well-being of those around you.

"Hence, you've been entrusted with so much more than many, and as such your abilities have grown in kind. As we improve ourselves, our mindsets, and more, and as we go along in life, we too will receive further updates, like yours. You are starting off nearly perfect and with the full spectrum of abilities available, many of which you can and will learn as you go along in life. There are many other capabilities we will all learn as they are conceived of and implemented, but we'll train you to learn how to control and use many of them as we enter the Virtual Universe. Step-by-step and easy does it, as they say; you'll learn and grasp so much more. Physiological optimizations tied-in with your right brain are only minor side-effects of all of this."

Vesha paused Yesha, thrilled with the idea that her lifelong dream friend was actually a part of her expressing herself beautifully and uniquely, while also respecting her own life-long sense of how she imagined herself. "I can't believe it! I don't understand. I mean I appreciate all of this," she waved her hands up and down her perfect body, "How do you know I named her Sky?"

Yesha grabbed a nearby portable mirror so Vesha could see. Just below her left breast was the angel, and right on the underside of her breast flowed the name, Sky. "Pretty obvious, don't you think?

"Your artistic artwork will change over time, but she kind of flies around a bit, and she does it ever-so artistically. Now, please understand, that there are many other aspects of your physiology and neurology integrated in a manner that affords you autonomously natural aspects that don't require conscious thought on your part, but you also have much more control with some of the most intriguing of things, such as manipulation of eyesight, healing, pain tolerance, and other adjustments.

"You're still a human and a biological miracle if you ask me, and you are not your right brain alone, but because of Sky, you have abilities that most would envy if they knew of them. To top that off, I don't think anyone can say they've seen anything or anyone more aesthetically pleasing as you, and soon we will both learn how your neurology works, now that you are awake.

"I'd imagine it will amaze us in much the same way as your physique." Yesha said as she motioned her hands—waving them over Vesha's entirely nude and exquisite frame, impressed with her, yet also so happy that everything turned out so well. "Our technology was something of diligence, but we grew to appreciate the beautiful set of enhancements that happened to appear automatically, through the artwork like a silent movie, and after much deliberation, we decided the mind's art was optimal too and left it free for expression.

"The artwork is not an arrangement of tattoos, it is a part of your cellular makeup as expressed by your mind. The highlights, your floral scent are all expressions of you, and whenever your body heals, you'll see iridescent sparkles all over your skin, kind of like shiny little diamonds glowing. When you blush, you'll glow a little bit as well."

"You're glowing a little bit, Yesha," said Vesha Celeste with a slight smile, but kidding around. She knew Yesha was being professional, was proud of her work, and she was grateful. Vesha didn't sense anything funny, the whole ambiance of it all was innocent and gracious.

"I know," said Yesha. "I'm just so happy that everything turned out so well. I mean, the lacy black and white sort of doily and mandala-like pattern with Sky's expressive artistry, all up and down your left shoulder and down to your left thigh and feet, combined with the colors of your eyes and your hair, are all in sync. The aesthetic of each feature complements the other. You are amazing in every way. You invoke beauty and charm, yet authority and loyalty, and I thank the stars. Do you know you used one of your new skills not too long ago?"

"I did? What did I do?"

"You talked about how society needs to appreciate the beauty of the human body, the wonder of evolution and the advancements we've achieved, to increase well-being and quality of life. You then thanked

Eliza and everyone in Pathway for bringing you back so beautifully."

Vesha appreciated Yesha's genuine compliment, "Thank you and everyone for doing this for me. I suppose I owe some gratitude to Sky, she has been my kindred spirit for quite some time.

"So, it seems that we apparently have telepathic transceiver capabilities, too? I suppose in my state of dementia, there must have been a variety of upgrades, developments, and advancements that were brought about that I didn't retain or remember. My focus was mostly on recalling the memories of my family and friends, and all who had shown me love in my lifetime. I hope you don't mind, and I digress, I must say—and I don't want to sound too narcissistic or egotistical, but I do appreciate all of this. I could gaze at myself for hours since there is so much that is artistic and captivating, and right now I am overwhelmed and impressed; it is nice to share that with someone. Thank you so much for doing so well for me."

While gazing in the mirror at her fullness of beauty for just a little longer, Vesha asked, "You were saying I was out for two years and that there is more training to be had. I don't recall too much regarding the Virtual Universe since I was an honorary member at the time, but you hinted that we will need to go there for my more extensive training. When do we begin?"

"You were out for exactly two years, to the day. It is December 25th, 2018. Yes, you'll find out much more about everything in a more experiential sort of way, and in a little bit within the Virtual Universe. We can begin as soon as you'd like." Forgetting momentarily about the fact that Vesha was still undressed, because her nudity actually seemed unusually innocent and even normal in this particular environment, free of harsh or impure personalities or intentions, she beckoned, "Come. Let me show you the Virtual Universe. We'll be able to do some amazing training there and show you a robustly historic briefing when we interface with our biopods. At least, that's our first priority for now," said Yesha, with her typically calm demeanor and giddy intent.

"Like this?" Vesha fluttered her hands over her exposed and upgraded body. Vesha turned away from the mirror after looking one last time and then toward Yesha, who was impressed just a little more with the beauty and awesomeness of her gorgeous physical exterior.

Yesha, with a very approving smile, thought to herself for a fraction of a microsecond, "*I can't believe this is the first time we have actually revived someone who has passed away. We had a lot of healings and upgrades, but this is a full-on resurrection and a complete success! ...And, oh my, I'm speechlessly awestruck; she looks incredible!*"

Vesha picked up on something. It was as if Yesha had whispered to her. She recalled their conversation about telepathy, and then brushed it off knowing she would learn more about her powers soon.

As Vesha released her mind, knowing that Yesha had talked to her using telepathy, she saw a space-age-like outfit—a black, thick, rubbery, yet cloth-like material, with artistic colorations glimmering in streams of detailed and sewn-in embroidery, matching the colors of the highlights in her hair, her body's artwork, and the irises of her eyes. As she put it on, she noticed the embroidery was seamlessly sewn to the stretchy yet oddly comfortable contraption that was made-to-fit just for her.

It had been hanging at the level of her gaze, so she had gently pulled the uniform down off the garment fixture on the door and began to put it on. Vesha pulled her legs through, covered her perfect, gloriously perky, and ample bosoms, one at a time, hiding the artistic imagery, and thinking she'd need a little help with the back she asked, "Can you help me with this? This must be an outfit fitted just for me, since it fits me like a glove; it would seem that I may need you to get the zipper, or whatever it is back there, please?"

The bathroom door had been opened and Yesha had been observing her through the doorway, so she didn't need to reach too far to zip her up. Nonetheless, Yesha responded, "Your uniform does not have a zipper."

She motioned for her to turn her head so Vesha could see her back in the mirror, "It is made out of smart material and is designed to give you maximum comfort. Your smartsuit provides a mixture of just the right amount of moisture, flowery mind-controlled scent, and temperature control, as well as physical strength and dexterity. The sophisticated technology in your smartsuit augments your commanding yet easing appearance of beauty, respect, joy, and peace. The micro-nanos that are within it work with your mind, so you can seal it shut or adjust your wardrobe as desired.

"Both sealing and wardrobe mechanisms are triggered by your neural activity when you think, *'Seal my suit.'* In many cases, clothes already worn are converted to smartsuits via the biopod, but you are our first individual in the known history of humanity, and proven scientifically, to be resurrected, so for you, it's different.

"You'll only need one of these suits. This tech will allow you to encode it with compartmentalizations within your mind to give you any look you need at any moment. Plus, it is self-washing, providing you top-notch hygiene, no more need for waxing of unwanted hairs or needing a shower after something intense, because your nanos will kick in, and so will your smartsuit. Simply think of what you need done as far as wardrobe is concerned, and it will be done. All of that, while giving you the aromatic scent you prefer, given any situation.

"Although, all things considered, if you ask me, there never is something as amazing as slipping out of everything for a nice, large, warm bubble bath. But I digress; sometimes, in the regular world, you'll want to look more professional, and at other times you'll want to wear a bikini for the beach.

"There are codes built into your clothing's neuroware that will allow it to take on the appearance you need, which can be activated merely on thought—eventually all of this will be second nature to you, and you'll want to ensure your appearance doesn't change right in front of John Q. Public. In the not-too-distant future, you may just want to look as creative as your heart desires."

As she spoke, Yesha's blouse and skirt turned into a revealing see-through dark negligée which accentuated her ample curves, and highlighted the natural colorings of her skin, eyes, and hair. Through the negligée, Vesha saw a hint of Yesha's tattoo-like artistry playing out before her, images circulating up and down her dermis as if it were a movie. This happened, but just for a few seconds, because like that her appearance returned to the professional yet attractive one, she'd had on before. "Just like that, and in a snap, you can change." Vesha had seen her uniform seal up just moments before as Yesha had explained everything, right after her telepathic command.

"That outfit you had on for a split second and your right-mind artistry, that was hot date material," Vesha laughed. "I didn't realize you would have artwork like that too. You also used your telepathy to seal up my uniform on command. I suppose you could peel it off if you wanted to as well? I'm kidding. I still can't get over how amazing all of this is!" Vesha said, she was good friends with Yesha, had been for years, and appreciated that she had a good sense of humor. She wanted to show off a bit longer, maybe if her husband from her previous life had been there, she would. She didn't mind Yesha being an observer since there was a lot of detail in the artwork and there seemed to be no rush. She was impressed that Yesha must have been affected by many of the same artwork benefits.

"These odd feelings I am having—why am I buzzing with intensity, and why does it feel so good? This is the bomb!" Vesha was starting to feel like one of the younger adults she had known and using the vocabulary she had heard them use seemed to come more naturally as the moments continued. *"I wonder what Yesha's artwork is like and I wonder if she has a unique alter-ego like I do, like Sky?"* Vesha was using one of her new gifts again, without realizing she had happened to be targeting Yesha for a very private conversation, but she knew in time, maybe if they went swimming on a beach somewhere, Yesha would show her. Vesha loved the new details, imaginative expressions, and being optimized.

"Oh? I'd show you more, but I won't for now. Maybe we can hit up a beach later on, but we don't have that on our list of things to do today," Yesha told Vesha through her mental link. She then climbed deeper into her mind and thoughts, trying to get back to task, *"We need to get you trained in the Virtual Universe,"* thought Yesha, as she smiled at Vesha. She had the innocent look of 'I know what you were thinking, and that's cool,' and then both seemed ready to get Vesha's training under way.

"I'm liking this telepathy we have. Goodbye cell phones!" Vesha laughed, and her skin blushed a little with a crystalline glow, as she realized her body was adjusting to allow her new gifted ability to set in for good. She then asked, "How much, exactly, has gone on since I put my head on my pillow? It seems to me like it was just a few hours ago that I hugged my family goodbye. Maybe my mind is still processing everything, but I honestly still have no idea what day it is or where I am, but," she paused, "I remember. Yeah, you said it is two years later. But, where are we then? Oh, wait, you said we are in Massachusetts, at the Melrose Campus? Okay, I see you're looking at me funny. Go ahead and enlighten me, please?" Vesha was trying to remember all they'd talked about, but clearly her neuro nanos were working and she was left just a little confused, temporarily. Yesha knew that.

"You are correct, Vesha. We are at the Pathway Campuses, but I didn't tell you that we are deep within the

Earth, about fifty miles down, but as safe as can be. I also didn't tell you I am currently the leader and president of Pathway since Eliza is serving in the Senate. She is the leader of the Universal Party and is still connected with us via her neural link. She would visit us right now, but she is currently in deliberation at the Senate. Even though it is a holiday and two years exactly from the day you passed away. Eliza wanted to be here, but the Senate had some work that needed to be done, regardless, so her link is on but dampened right now. She honestly would have been here if she could have helped it, but I am here, plus I am sure you know by now that I, like she, was just as excited to see my dear and brilliant friend!

"We'd been working with your physiological and neurological aspects for a long time, to the point of which we had on multiple occasions triggered every possible and conceivable physiological response before waking you, and when all responses seemed to ensure perfection, we activated your mind. We also did so with you in a replica of your domicile at the Princeton Assisted Living center, with quite a few minor adjustments to get you thinking, which you did, and successfully I might add. As you began to awake, I started knocking on your door. Remember the neuro-transceivers and software applications we installed on all of our phones at Pathway several years ago?"

"Oh, yes, I do recall that now. It's coming back to me. Since I'm new to the neuro nanos, my guess is that I get a little confused as they are running and linking my newly-discovered abilities and using them." Vesha then explained with the newfound clarity her gifted mind had bequeathed her with, "You were able to gather my final moments, all of my brain activity, and even capture my sense of self, using what Eliza's technology had been set up to do, with Pathway's crew of scientists?"

Impressed with Vesha's returning sense of short-term memory, navigating away from the signs of dementia that had taken her away from the world, and pleased with her increasing abilities toward critical thinking, as her nanos clearly indicated, Yesha continued for Vesha and went into more detail, "In fact we did.

"The moment you passed away we were all notified via our neural links, and at the same time your last moments of thought, as well as the rest of your physiological and neurological information, were backed up and automatically sent to Pathway's Twelve Database Moons. As this happened, the Twelve Database Moons essentially sounded off like an alarm in our minds, and we received all of your final and complete bits of information—your thoughts, your memories, your hopes, your dreams, your knowledge, your biological construct, your wisdom, and of course your moments with Sky.

"We then synced all of your information, including your actual consciousness, to a lifeless mold of you that we had synthesized based upon an optimized form of your own DNA, similar to the way in which we each had previously data-based our DNA when we began Pathway eight years ago.

"The body you are in now, not long ago, while we were working on you, had been imbued with nano-technology and was constantly checked, optimized, and improved upon in an anesthetized and 'off' state, save for the cells themselves which communicated their necessary functions. Just as we had previously agreed upon, we were able to complete every aspect of you in two years.

"Knowing how this is done now, we will now be able to do this for anyone else in a matter of a few minutes. Since you were the first to be reawakened after passing away, we took our time, ran every diagnostic, and did every check. We developed a systematic set of procedures for this same sort of resurrection in the future, depending on how all of this goes through.

"When everything was ready, we activated the opsin-nano-neural-links and turned you on. Thus far, everything has gone splendidly." Yesha smiled, noticing Vesha's mind was grasping all that she was explaining, *"I'm proud of you, Vesha. You are understanding and picking up everything quicker than the rest of us did,"* she continued, "You woke up with full control of your body. You also have naturally expected and automated responses, like breathing, which is no longer necessary, but we still use that function to keep the public from suspecting such, or getting creeped out, among other things. For you, a second had passed as if nothing had happened, for us it'd been exactly two years.

"Even though Eliza had just become a US Congressional Representative for our beloved state of Massachusetts, she, who had been very close, and I worked to optimize you and bring you back for quite some time. For a couple of years, to be exact, and together with Amber Blythe, Erin Carter, Najem Grace, Jasmine Belle, James Cooper, and other dear friends of Pathway, to include Eliza and me, we were able to optimize your DNA, and now you have these results, right before your eyes.

"Eliza would have been here too, today, but as you already know, she is currently dealing with pressing issues in the Senate, as well with the Press and the established scientific communities. Everything seems to be pretty well locked-down though. Everyone that can be here, who was involved with this entire process or any part of it, is here now, but out of view—since we didn't want to overwhelm you with too many changes or oddities at once. I was unanimously voted to awaken you, but of course, you know I already wanted to. Nevertheless, the Pathway community is observing our interactions and has been working closely with us tracking your progress intently and so far, you are doing phenomenally.

"This is your body, and as I have already suggested, and you seem to understand, you have both neuro and bio nanos roaming throughout your system. They are continually taking free radicals, bio-waste, dead cells, and harmful debris and converting them into useful proteins, cellular constructs, optimized organisms, max-capacity neurons, and providing the ideal fluctuation of energy for optimal use of your mind and body. They stand at the ready, should anything catastrophic ever occur, to heal you to complete and full health and memory.

"Your corpus callosum, prefrontal cortex, as well as all of your other cortices and deep brain regions, are actually interfaced by using your neuro-nanos to act as a transceiver. This allows your mind to send thoughts, ideas, dreams, memories, the whole gamut, wirelessly between every aspect of you and our Twelve Database Moons, enabling you to communicate and so much more with anyone you wish to link with, if they have been optimized and trained in the Virtual Universe.

"Since you recently reawakened, I currently have complete access to your neural activity, until you have completed your training for the sake of the safety and security of all involved including yourself. With so much going on, we didn't want to risk serious anomalies."

When Vesha heard this, she was slightly alarmed, yet she didn't feel too embarrassed. She examined the thoughts she had allowed to pass through her mind and sensed that all was okay with everyone and even Yesha.

"Don't worry, you're quite okay, and the feelings of gratitude are mutual in every sense. Get used to being flirted with though, since we'll both have an ultra-attractive effect on people for the foreseeable future, and it is a nice perk," Yesha continued, to put her at ease. Every word she said flourished with purity.

"Encrypted within your unique neural code is the ability to control what you share with others, it also serves to allow us to currently monitor you with your own unique identification since you were only recently revived. This also provides Pathway your vital signs, all while it actually protects your privacy. It gives you access to the locations within our organization and throughout the solar system using jump gates and teleportation, as well as to the different matrices within the Virtual Universe. It allows you to learn as much as you'd like, to gain associated experience and upgrade—as upgrades become available.

"When you're ready, we can sync up to the matrices and go to the Virtual Universe. From there we can share a journey through Eliza's life as well as the lives and experiences of a few other individuals critical to the growth of Pathway. We'll do this so you can have a more complete understanding of what it is that has happened while you were otherwise engaged and away. You'll learn what led to all of this in the first place, as well as what is planned for the future."

Vesha thought about all that Yesha had explained for a few brief seconds, and she approved of every aspect of her transition, had no problem if James or other scientists caught a glimpse during the process, and accepted her new reality. Vesha was excited to explore the Virtual Universe. First, however, she was curious about the possibilities of exploring the real world in her new body, "Would you be bothered if we went for a stroll out in the public, first? You know, to stretch the muscles and capture the sites and the sounds? Unless you have objections or other plans, I wouldn't mind showing off."

Yesha smiled, was proud of her newfound confidence, then stood, looked down, tapped her foot, and waited for Vesha's next response.

Vesha was willing to follow Yesha's guidance, and Yesha knew it. Vesha considered everything. Yesha was probably already well-versed on what was going on and had conveyed this in more ways than one.

The advancements, the legalities, the so-called ethical concerns prevalent in society and governance, which had nothing to do with ethics whatsoever, and well, she had essentially just resurrected her after all. It was most likely that all of this was still covert, but legitimate, so she was willing to press on with her request. Plus, she kind of looked at Yesha as sort of her own young and beautiful guardian angel with an additionally kindred spirit-like overtone. "I understand, Yesha. When can we go to the Virtual Universe for my training?"

"Follow me," said Yesha, with a pleasant sense of approval and happiness. Then Vesha felt something in her mind, and knew it was Yesha who seemed to say, "*Open.*"

Yesha led her down the hallway of her home to a door that she hadn't realized was there before—the corridor had pretty much been a dead end beyond her bedroom and bathroom, and then the door became unsealed and visible. Like that, it opened right before her eyes to reveal a very fascinating view of a room with a gentle white glow and another set of doors.

Okay," said Vesha, "I know that one of the additional optimizations we have is telepathy, I figured it out, you explained it when I forgot again, and then I recalled it all after my neuro nanos finished updating my capacities as it related to my upgrades, but it appears we also have telekinesis. I'm still trying to grasp the reality of it." Vesha thought for a second, felt the upgrade work its way through her system, and then continued, "Sweet deal! I suppose we only have telekinesis, for now, with things that are programmed to pick up our neural identification and then our telepathic orders. You and Eliza had a lot more figured out than I realized, I mean, look at you... you are mind-numbingly gorgeous and ultra-intelligent!"

"*Yes, Vesha, I was optimized, or we, I and Eliza, optimized ourselves the day we were one-hundred percent sure this technology was spot on. We didn't want to take the risk that would have come with the loss of the technology, nor did we want to be weak in the face of any of those who might suggest we do otherwise. She set hers ten years ago to maintain a static age of twenty-two, even though she is currently thirty-eight, but she did so in a way that wouldn't be obvious, and I have been a static age for quite a few years. People still haven't caught on to the fact that we're no spring chickens, per-say, but I still look like I did when I was twenty-five, and I'm forty-one."* Yesha noticed that Vesha was still kind of looking around with a bemused air of wonder, her eyes and neck cocked to pick up the audio transmission sent by voice, but she was catching on quickly, and she smiled.

Despite Vesha's disbelief, Yesha could tell that she was capable of perceiving what she was telling her mentally. That ability took many others quite a bit longer to practice and achieve. In many cases, a few hours of practice in the Virtual Universe was almost required, and Vesha hadn't even been there yet—she was actually pretty quick, all things considered.

"Were you able to hear me?" asked Yesha, "I know you were going to ask. I know there has been a lot loaded upon you all at once. Even with an optimized mind, things take practice, study, and more practice to perfect and retain. Yes, I can actually link up wirelessly to your mind as we stand or walk or even chat, and I can pick up on a few other things; as per our Pathway honorary member contract, once we've each been optimized, we can link up to each other and converse—as you say, telepathically. I was telling you that earlier. Do you believe me now?"

"Yes, of course, I believe you, Yesha. So, how do I talk to you like that?" asked Vesha.

"Well, you actually have on three occasions already, and I'm sure you'll recall that soon enough. But it will be easier to show you more clearly once we have entered the Virtual Universe or the matrices—and don't worry, Eliza had to show me in the Virtual Universe too.

"No one thus far has picked up on telepathy near as fast as you have. Everyone else found out how to, well after they were in the matrices, and we're just getting ready to go there. That said, it is okay that they took longer because it takes a while to consciously connect with those regions of the brain, but again, you are unique in a wonderful way," said Yesha.

"Okay," Yesha pointed down the hallway, "*Open,*" and she continued through the other set of doors, after the final set opened before her, "This smart door, right here, activates when we issue the command 'open,' within our minds. It takes a while to be familiar with all of the commands and how to control the different areas of the brain. In this case, we use the prefrontal cortex at a subconscious level, which is said to be virtually impossible. That's why we need to go into the Virtual

Universe via the biopods, which are located in that room, for training.

"The reprogrammable matter technology within the infrastructure of the Pathway Melrose Campuses allows the doors to become visible as we interact with our neuro nanos. Our neural activity and the security system transceivers near the doors open when we issue the command, 'open.' We do that subconsciously while directing our thoughts to the door, which is designed with smart technology, and when we do, they will open upon instant neural identification recognition."

Yesha continued, "Through these doors are our biopods. This is your Earth domicile, and we each have several biopods in our homes. These biopods allow us to be in a sleep-like state, while we're synced-in with the matrices in the Virtual Universe. Having a few of them in our home affords a few friends to come along with us for a shared experience. A biopod gives any individual within them an added set of safety, security, and protection protocols while we are 'away' or 'out' and they also give our physiology a bit of a break.

"We can link to the Matrices standing, walking, or traveling in any manner as well, but it is safest to use the biopods, so we don't run into things or make spectacles of ourselves. Furthermore, our biopods interact with our nanos, stimulate our senses and tactile responses, and give us a real sense of doing what we do there and being where we are, virtually giving us muscle memory, all the while keeping us optimized both physiologically and neurologically. In a beautiful sense of difference to the surreal nature and residual forgetting of a dream before our neurological and physiological optimizations, now that we are enhanced, we will be able to remember everything."

Vesha finally grasped what she had been through during her awakening, began to understand in-depth what she was seeing, and quickly made sense of what she was hearing. Her neuro nanos were kicking into high gear with their seamless processes of optimizing her mind, and everything seemed to have a profound ability to make sense on so many levels.

Finally finding her mind give way to a new sense of clarity of her past, Vesha spoke, "I remember now like it was yesterday. Eliza talked about all of this when she was giving her first Pathway Industries convention speech in 2012, and she said something about how each of these technologies was involved in one way or another.

"I don't think that I was part of Pathway for very long after that before my dementia started kicking into high gear. But I do recall you were at my dear Jillian's funeral. You paid your respects and offered me consolation, so I thank you for that." Vesha paused in thought for a small moment, "All of those technologies were actually developed by you and Eliza. They were confirmed and improved through Pathway, and they are currently ready for proliferation worldwide yet remain on standby and only in use by Pathway members until legalities are right. These are the biopods, right here—each of which works as a secure Virtual Universe interface?"

Vesha looked at what she saw with awe and then continued, but this time she seemed to discover that it was easy to mentally flex her neural cortices and grasped how to telepathically speak to Yesha, *"I've got this Yesha. The two white beds with hard-shelled covers that are spacious enough to lie on, and have doors that can be brought down manually, or most likely using a mental command to enclose them, help to provide our physiology and neurology additional optimizations, safety, and security while our minds are interfaced elsewhere."*

"Oh yes, and so much more," Yesha responded, while actually quite impressed. "Here, take a seat and lay down. Once you are comfortably settled in and ready for the cover to enclose you, pull the cover down and think the words, *Link 1, 2, 3.*" Vesha heard Yesha's command as clear as day but in her mind. After issuing that command, the hardcover closed over her. She knew that Yesha had telepathically commanded her biopod cover to shut, and that had registered to her own mind from within Yesha's. Just as Yesha had explained before, she had temporary control over Vesha's neural links because she was in training. Vesha then concentrated, focused on her mind again, her mouth, her words, and felt them all unite.

"Can you hear me, Yesha?"

"Yes, I can," Yesha thought, with a smile of approval on her face, unseen by Vesha's physical eyes, but seen as plain as day within her mind, plus she could hear the assuring, gracious, giddy, and comforting tone of her mental voice. *"You're a quick learner, Vesha. No one has learned this fast, well, except Eliza. She showed me how to in the Matrices.*

"Are you ready? We can both trigger our biopods, now that we're settled in. Once we say, 'Link 1, 2, 3', we need to set it for real-world time and then Virtual Universe time. In our case, we'll be in there for five minutes of real-world time, and about twenty years or more, adjusting as needed while in there, of Virtual Universe time. We will be going on journeys and covering a lot of information. We will be experiencing life through our eyes, so you can see some of what Pathway has accomplished since you passed away. You will also be able to look through the eyes and minds of many others while learning so much more. We will train you on every type of history you can imagine, on many more of the sciences, and on more of your new abilities."

"For five minutes?" Vesha asked out loud and somewhat in disbelief, but it was because her neuro nanos were kicking in again, adjusting her telepathic powers. When she spoke, it was barely audible through both of their enclosed biopods, but with Yesha's optimized mind and hearing she understood every word she said. Vesha would soon learn that Yesha was linked to her and could hear her, even if she muttered something seemingly inaudible under her breath.

Yesha paused, "Yes, my renewed, gifted, and dear friend, five minutes. Say 'Link 1, 2, 3, 5, 20' in your mind. Many of the questions that you're pretty much already answering due to your optimized intuition, right now, will be so much easier to retain and understand there. Do you see your glow? Look at your hand. That is because both your physiology and neurology are working to make sense of so much at once, and you are receiving collective updates based on your comprehension.

"The upgrades that are currently available are being released to you in kind. Once we sync up, everything else will make sense to you more clearly, and both your comprehension and capabilities will compound exponentially. The processes of application, efficiency, clarity, raw knowledge and skill will be multiplied using time dilation, and you will gain experiential wisdom. Although you've been keen enough to figure a lot out already, there is so much more, so, *are you ready?*"

Chapter 08: A New Journey

Database Moon Archive, Celestial-Sol Entry Date: 2018 December 25. The following is the continuation of Vesha Celeste's experiences, training, and journeys in the Virtual Universe. Sky is introduced in virtual corporeal form as Vesha's friend to Yesha. Although Sky is an alter ego of Vesha's right brain, Sky is powerful enough to be her own benevolent and highly capable entity. Yesha shows them Eliza, who is meditating. Database Moon Archive input made by Yesha Alevtina, President of Pathway Industries, from 2015-2022.

Vesha thought about the soon-to-begin journey throughout the Virtual Universe for a few milliseconds and then realized that with her new optimizations she wasn't currently hungry, and she didn't feel the need to use the restroom. Focusing again on the same three senses, she pushed out mentally and conversed with Yesha mind to mind, *"I am ready. Let's do this."* Vesha then continued, *"...Link 1, 2, 3, 5, 20"*

And just like that, Vesha felt every single sensory gland within her body contort, almost convulse, and then everything began to relax and buzz with an almost euphoric sense of ecstasy. A few moments passed, and she felt completely normalized, in control again, yet within a whole new environment. She then felt a very amplified and spectacular sense that her understanding of all that she had perceived and was now receiving into her mind was growing and becoming increasingly clear in a very exponential manner, just as Yesha had promised.

As she let this altogether new reality take its hold, Vesha looked around with her eyes. She felt as though she was peering out at what was before her in a very rational and stable manner, and then she saw a pond with a little waterfall teeming with coy fish. Surrounding the pool of water was a series of flowering and aroma-giving plants and at the top of the waterfall in the center of the big bath of water stood a beautiful statue of an angel overlooking its surroundings. Vesha was amazed at the sense of peace and solitude that she felt, and then suddenly wondered if she was alone. Looking around, she saw Yesha to her right and to her astonishment Sky was to her left.

"This is beautiful, Yesha and Sky. Where are we?" Sky hovered slightly above both of them in silence and turned her gaze from Yesha to Vesha. Apparently, Vesha's dream angel, Sky, already knew where they were, but she listened intently to hear Yesha's response anyway.

"We're in the area of Eliza's property just behind her estate home, or a virtual and realistic replica of it, in every sense, down to single particles, within the quantum computers and the Twelve Database Moon Virtual Matrix Mainframes. When we go that way, we will see the Virtual Universe depiction of Eliza's house," she briefly paused. Then, pointing toward a large white-stoned building surrounded with beautiful columns, while looking more enigmatic than ever, *"This is actually her home and her meditating moments as she experienced them the day Agent Epstein called her, in 2010. This was when she received the okay to start a relationship with the US Government and build Pathway's Federal Liaison Office, in Washington DC, based on the details of her authored and published book, 'Pathway to the Stars.'*

"We'll learn about that very soon.

"Eliza is sitting inside and meditating, and if you would like to experience her moments of reflection, follow me," Yesha said. Vesha and Sky followed her willingly. They walked away from the pond and toward the back entrance of Eliza's home. Leading to it was a stone pathway, encompassed by flowers. Vesha saw Yesha as she vanished like a ghost through the door, and then Sky followed Vesha, not too far behind. She then passed through the door in the same way, without needing to open it. Vesha looked around and noticed that when they

entered the home, they were inside a spacious and beautifully decorated living room. She drifted her gaze around the beautiful internal aspects of this historical structure, and then she saw Eliza.

To her recollection, of all the people she had ever met or known, Eliza was the most beautiful being that she had ever beheld. Her nearly white and golden hair, with pink weaves throughout her mid-length hair, glowed, in some ways like her dream angel's, Sky. Her eyes were shut, and she was clearly meditating. Vesha then heard a beautiful compilation of music. She asked Yesha what it was, who then told her that it was from Jens Gad's "Glass House." The music played in the air as if floating, pulsating, and moving magic through the soul. Meanwhile, Tyson, her brindle Boxador dog, lay there beside her curled up in a cuddly fifty-pound ball as Eliza was lost in thought. Sky looked at Vesha, then Yesha, and then demurely toward Eliza.

Vesha spoke up, *"Will Eliza be able to see or hear us? Will she know that we are here? I see she is meditating, but wait, as you said, this is in her past. How can this be? Why is it that I get the sense that somehow, I may already know or have access to all of the answers to my questions?"*

"You are connected to the Twelve Database Moons, the Multi-Matrix Mainframe, and you are connected mentally to me, Sky, and anyone else within

the Virtual Universe who has granted you access to their thoughts. You'll be surprised at how much clarity on everything you'll have as we move forward, observe, and listen—learning in fullness will come to the surface so much easier here." Yesha's eyes were closed in peaceful enjoyment of the ambiance, as she spoke. She had settled next to Eliza and Tyson and seemed to begin a thoughtful meditation process too.

It was as if a thick amalgamation of memories swirled in the air before Vesha. Clearly, there was a deep connection between Yesha, Eliza, Tyson, and this entire location—from the pond outside, to the couch in the living room, and beyond.

Yesha then opened her now bright and glowing eyes and continued, *"This simulation of Eliza is from her mind both three and eight years ago. In all actuality, Eliza and her current mental reality will sync with the latest updates of and to her mind, and she will know we were here and have complete awareness of everything we do and say in here, soon enough. She will be able to interact with us if we wish. At any point, you can choose to compartmentalize or privatize your thoughts, dreams, actions, and we can leave the Virtual Universe if you feel uncomfortable. We are here to learn and train, and if you are okay with it, we will continue."*

"I am fine. I am rather enjoying all of this and taking it all in. This is amazing."

"Well, let's continue. We can talk to Eliza now if you wish, or we can talk to her later. No matter when we choose to speak with her, right now she is, in physical form, on the Senate Floor. So, even though she can feel our emotions, which we will play out for her as if they are briefly-correlated images of thoughts and waves in her mind that are encoded in a unique mental flavor to let her know they aren't her own thoughts through her neural link, she will soon be updated in near real-time. Even though she has muted most everything for the purpose of focus there, she will catch up with us after the deliberation. Right now, I will answer a few questions, maybe show you a few things, and then we'll follow her through her self-reflection.

"There is a lot of important nuance to what she has experienced in life, and it will help if I can give you sufficient historical context, as well as the proper updates to your cognitive framework, and the training you will need. Ultimately, it can change a life if a person can experience another's within their own mind—and in particular within her mind since she is the highest-level genius, healer, and empath in the world, and quite possibly within our known Universe. Our minds will meld together with hers and doing so will help us all to understand each other completely," Yesha said, with a Virtual Universe smile.

"Forgive me for this, and I've meant to ask you, Vesha, both you and Eliza have been through quite a few tragic events. Would you mind sharing that with me?" asked Vesha, in the most understanding of inquisitive tones possible. Vesha then noticed Yesha's smile and the peaceful and friendly understanding of her innocent intentions, and then Yesha looked down. As she did, her expressions began to take a more somber tone.

"We are close friends and have been ever since she was born, and a lot has happened that has led us to where we are now." Yesha then looked up at Sky, smiled, and then toward Vesha. Vesha saw Yesha's glowing, loving, and wise eyes—accentuating the beauty of the mixture of hazels, beiges, and greens radiating from her irises framed within thick black limbal rings, which suggested wisdom and youth. Yesha then continued, *"We've been through a lot together, have accomplished a lot together—much of which has yet to be revealed to the rest of the world. However, I had just turned three when I looked upon Eliza for the first time and saw as she opened her eyes not more than two minutes after she came to life. Even as a newborn she saw me in the room as if I were the only one there, looked toward me, and smiled. Those adorable big blue crystalline eyes were compelling, and I could tell, even with my three-year-old perceptions at the time with the clarity of that moment as if it took place yesterday, and by the immediate*

richness to her character, that right away she was destined for greatness. I also knew then that we were going to be kindred spirits, close to each other throughout life—we were going to be besties. Neither of us is currently in a relationship, and you'll understand why, soon enough—I can tell you now, but to experience it all is so much more profound. It won't always be that we are alone, but for now, our priorities are a big factor, and we have so much to do."

Sobered by Yesha's pause, Vesha knew something had happened, that even Yesha had private memories, and perhaps there was more she would learn or be willing to share later. Despite their neural connection, she wasn't quite sure what it was she was withholding. Yet, she sensed a well of respect growing within herself for the provision and evidence of privacy despite the openness of her mind. Something about the ability to share what one was willing to share increased her trust in all that she was experiencing, learning, and beholding.

While she was in the Virtual Universe and interfaced through her biopod, the nanos, no matter where she went, would heal any damage she might incur and carry out or repurpose any debris. She could feel her optimizations and the abilities of her updates and upgrades increasing as her mind released more synaptic and neural pathways to an increase in vibrant clarity and forged new and even stronger ones on any given subject.

Pondering on how all of this technology increasingly made sense, like that all of it began to unfold its internal mechanisms and purpose before her. Vesha realized the beauty of Eliza's and Yesha's internal discipline, their collective knowledge and wisdom, the intensity of their minds, and their sense of duty and responsibility. She also felt their pain and knew that they must have experienced a myriad of occasions where emotions ran very deep. They had both been through profound romance and pain in their lives. Vesha began to sense a willingness to share with Yesha the loss of her own husband and daughter, accompanied with an onslaught of dementia, each of which had caused her deep emotional pain. What helped her to get through it all with peace within had been the fact that Sky had helped her in her younger and later years. As far as Eliza and Yesha were concerned, Vesha still wasn't clear what it could be that left those yet-unhealed scars, but she sensed that the pursuit of their goals and their potential conclusions would mend them, and she found comfort in their determination to make right what was wrong in the world. She appreciated the fact that they shared an extraordinary set of experiences leading to a deep connection. Furthermore, Vesha could feel the beauty of what they shared beyond the ability to describe in words.

What Yesha and Eliza had was a unique bond, a genuine relationship, one of sisterhood, one of innocence, yet one of sadness and sorrow. In contrast, they shared a determination of joy and hope. She decided, for the time being, to shift the energy around them in a different direction, as she sensed a shared, yet belabored pain and a story of healing that went with it. However, she would only do that for a short period of time, because something about where they had been, the things they had done, and the visions they had seen intrigued her. *"I know you've both been through suffering, and I would imagine that despite your neurological healing capacities, there are still pains of loss and tragedy that will always be a part of us. Please only share what you can, when you feel the time is right. I know you are both wonderful young women and I can completely understand your need to hold back, especially when there are lessons to be learned when shared in the right context. That said, you mentioned something about a Virtual Universe Multi-Matrix Mainframe. What or where is that exactly?"*

Yesha responded reservedly, shifting her demeanor, and with almost a sense of happiness for the change in subject, she continued, *"Thank you, Vesha. I will share that with both you and Sky, but within an entirely different setting and context. You'll experience it in due time. In the meantime, since we're in here, I can show you the Mainframe, or better yet, one of the Twelve Database Moons. And, again, please don't worry, I'll share you the details of our history soon enough, but at the appropriate time."* Without warning, they started to rise up, through the roof of the house, and up into the nighttime sky.

Chapter 09: Magnificent View

Database Moon Archive, Celestial-Sol Entry Date: 2018 December 25. This is a continuation of Vesha's and Sky's experiences and some of Vesha's training and journeys in the Virtual Universe. After her entrance, Yesha allows Vesha and Sky to take in their new ambiance. Database Moon Archive input made by Yesha Alevtina, President of Pathway Industries, from 2015-2022.

The breeze of movement passed through Vesha's hair as if she were flying in the real world, living in a real environment, and with clouds breezing by. The brisk winds and the density of the particles of the atmosphere seemed to pass through her system as if to remind her that the Universe, if possible, still recognized her existence. She felt as if she was a form of radiation encoded with information, yet moving along unaffected, similar to quantum particles, such as neutrinos or other exotic and yet-to-be-discovered quanta—the types that Eliza had already discovered, and her mind was only beginning to conceive of and grasp. As she climbed through the stratosphere with Yesha at the lead and Sky at her side, it was more comfortable than sleeping in bed and within a wonderful dream. Arriving to and passing beyond microgravity, or the Virtual-Universe-simulation of it, Sky looked as though she was right at home. Like that, Sky had been up, up, and up through the clouds, and into the starry night, and Vesha was thrilled with this new and seemingly surreal reality, which wasn't so surreal after all. This was an experience she was truly going through.

Vesha looked out and began toying around with some newly-acquired abilities she had found. Discovering that if she adjusted her sight to mitigate the brilliance of the Sun, she could see so much more and ever-so clearly. Even though it had been several years since the use of her more complexed conscious brain activity, due to her mortal battles with dementia, now her brain was so robustly operational that she was beside herself. As she looked to Sky, she actually thought of the phrase, "beside herself," and chuckled. After sharing the thoughts of her mind with the other two, they all shared a laugh as they continued through the vacuum of space with subtle reminders of their reality.

Vesha was fixated upon one star with her eyes. She began to use that star to carry out the astrophysical calculations in her mind of where every other stellar and deep space object was, as well as where they happened to be, relative to Earth, along with each constellation asterism. Vesha knew what time of year it was, based on the Earth's orbit around the Sun and the geophysical aspects of the shadows upon the various mountains and landmass shapes, and then where the Andromeda Galaxy would be in open space. Vesha knew her observable Universe well, based on the stars seen and instantaneous triangulation of the northern and southern poles of the galactic disc and a host of other astrophysics formulas processing subconsciously and even numerically before her. The formulas she processed quickly opened her vision and she peered deeper than she had ever before.

In fact, as she looked around at each object, Vesha noticed a three-dimensional data display with all of the essential information of anything she focused on intentionally, and all, such that she could clearly see the object of concentration accompanied simultaneously and strategically placed for clarity with a detailed readout of the information her mind had requested. Vesha was suddenly breath-taken by the fact that she could navigate her vision around the icebergs and ice planets in the Oort Cloud and see Andromeda more clearly now than she had ever before seen it with the naked eye or with any of the most advanced telescopes available to her when she worked in the real world as an astrophysicist.

Vesha knew there were things she would continue to learn or even discover later, when it came to her focus on the different sensory systems and areas of her brain. With just one of her new capabilities, she could tune out the light, and with appropriately-coordinated cellular and nano overlays, correctly placed around the lenses of her eyes, factoring in bend, crystallization-manipulation, photon decoding and a variety of algorithms and physics formulas, she could see beautiful arrays of colors everywhere, from nebulae to star-forming regions, to rogue planets racing through space in the dark, and decipher their molecular and chemical makeup.

It donned on Vesha that the Virtual Universe itself was beckoning for her to try looking deeper. So, she did. With a more-focused concentration in other areas of deep space she saw supernovae, globular clusters of stars, elliptical galaxies, spiral galaxies, galactic superclusters, the dark matter holding them all together—the substance she had studied much of her life as an astrophysicist, and so much more. After looking out into the dark ever-so-deeply, she was able to see anywhere, from everywhere.

As Vesha focused within each neural-region of her mind, she dove deep into her occipital lobe and its associated areas of the brain, as well as several other helpful cortices, and for the first time ever, she saw galaxies of types that had never been named or documented throughout all of history, and then she experienced vision omnidirectionally and processed it all as if it were the norm. Her digital displays factored in gravitational lensing, triangulation, the Doppler Effect, and so much more in mere moments, and she had a full scope of the Universe around her in all of its complexities, relative to Earth. The colors out there were brilliant, and it was obvious that life existed out there, farther than humanity had ever been, through technology or any other means!

"Wow, Yesha and Sky, this is better than a dream! Instead of fleeting thoughts jumping around, it's as though there is this tied-in stability of the environment, yet I can focus wherever I would like, see farther than I ever have before, the nebulae, the galaxies, the supernovae, the rogue planets, all of the beautiful colors, and so much more, and it is amazing! I won't forget this or anything, because, unlike a dream, my environment isn't changing in an unstable manner, and my prefrontal cortex is as though it has expanded making sense of it all.

"To a certain extent, I see things differently, absorbing all of this information while accessing regions of my brain I never realized existed, but now I clearly realize these various regions do indeed exist and I can use them to hone the vast new options and capacities of my vision.

"Here we are; it's as if we are floating in space. I am here with you and Sky, and I can see any object I focus on clearer than I did while using the most advanced telescopes on Earth. I can see Lira, Cassiopeia, Orion, Perseus, Sagittarius, Pisces, and Pavo. I can zoom in on each star of each asterism, and deduce first, second, and third generation planetary systems. I am out in the near-absolute-zero temperature of space, and I'm not freezing. I'm not forgetting what I'm seeing, and I can see so much more.

"I'm looking around, yet I don't need to; I can see it all, and it is breathtakingly gorgeous. Seeing these locations in context, well, they make me curious to look even further. To add to this, the radiation and meteoroids don't have any negative effect on me, or us, whatsoever! It's wonderful being up here with you, Yesha, and my sweet dream angel, Sky; moments like these are beyond fantastic, especially when shared," Vesha and Sky looked around with her, while smiling and feeling a sweet release of freedom, and when they did, they all laughed in exhilaration and excitement.

"This is beautiful, Vesha and Yesha!" Said Sky.

Yesha smiled, allowing Vesha the time to enjoy what she saw for a few more marvelous and timeless moments, and then she responded. *"True and very astute on all accounts, both Vesha and Sky. There is a lot we can do, and I guarantee you, you have barely scratched the* surface. As you learn something and use it, you will not forget it, so there is a lot of wisdom in your observations. I am proud of you and your rapid progress!

"Now, I will also let you know, that when it comes to the fleeting thoughts we share, the more people we relate to and connect with, due to our neural links, the more rapidly we will learn and hone our new abilities. Interesting though, as we channel our skills, everything we can do will become mind-blowing in scope and awe, and as they say, the more of us linking just as we are now, the merrier we become. Among my favorite skills in the Virtual Universe or even when we wake up and practice them within the real world are telescopic vision, microscopic vision, omnivision, and buffeting the dangers of space with little effect upon our physiology.

"Still, there is more."

Chapter 10: Advances Abound

Database Moon Archive, Celestial-Sol Entry Date: 2018 December 25. The following is the continuation of Vesha Celeste's experiences and some of her training and journeys in the Virtual Universe. Yesha shows Vesha and Sky the Twelve Database Moons and many of Eliza's, Yesha's, James', and many other scientists of Pathway's remarkable, lovely, and breathtaking accomplishments. Database Moon Archive input made by Yesha Alevtina, President of Pathway Industries, from 2015-2022.

Yesha continued speaking after shifting her gaze, *"There are so many stunning and spectacular aspects about what we can see so far away, but sometimes it is just as beautiful and awesome to bring our focus in and see that which is nearby. Did you know, we can essentially fly to any location in the Universe that has ever been digitized or triangulated by these Twelve Database Moons that revolve around the Earth like satellites, and we can see and go pretty much everywhere, anywhere, and anytime? Our minds are synced with these large moon-like data centers using the most robust and state-of-the-art equipment. The sensory and protective transceiving systems and high-tech quantum computers are the most advanced of any others that have ever been built in the history of humanity. Together, they act as faster-than-light transceivers, using a variety of exotic quantum factors to jump instantly between the biopods, our neural transmissions between each other, and our bio and neuro-nanos for thought, shared-experiences, healing, learning, excitement, you name it—and they are synced to every place like this..."* As Yesha pointed, Vesha and Sky saw Earth's Moon, and then they saw another moon.

It was much smaller, but it was still magnificent, huge, gargantuan, and full of intrigue and luminosity, and it appeared to be three-hundred miles in diameter, based on Vesha's digital display!

"We are orbiting just on the outside of the *gravitational pull of our Moon, or what we sometimes call Selene, so, between Selene, and what are called, LaGrange Points 1 and 2," said Yesha. "This small moon and about eleven others like it are orbiting our Earth in a sophisticated array and tangent and are for all sakes and purposes more advanced than any construct made by humanity in the real world and are cloaked to the public eye, and thus are practically invisible. People* cannot see them by just looking up at the sky or scanning with conventional radars, sensory systems, or telescopic technologies. These satellites, which have more capacity and capability than all of the other satellites combined, have the latest in high-invisibility cloaking.

"Japanese scientists had been working on this technology for years, and they were doing a remarkable job. It was Eliza, however, who cracked the invisibility code a couple of years before the formation of Pathway and applied it as Pathway grew to every vulnerable and covert advancement she came up with. She did this to maximize our ability to protect humanity from the malicious use of any of the tech. Eliza ensured safety mechanisms were in place before the brewers of uncontrolled chaos or overmuch quantities of greed, selfishness, hatred, toxicity, and prejudice had an opportunity to grasp, understand, manipulate and use them for means that have nothing to do with the preservation of life, its longevity, or the well-being of humanity or life itself. It's a simple combination of undetectable multi-spectrum laser sensors, cameras, and digital pixilations, and particles that the established sciences have yet to discover. Look over there!"

Yesha pointed toward several magnificent and gleaming cities sprawling the dark side of the Moon. "These cities are but a few of many. They span the solar system with a total of twenty-thousand cities that can *provide high-quality living for at least ten-million families, with capacity for growth, and can only be seen by those who have been optimized and interfaced for further training within the Virtual Universe. The designs for these high-tech cities, with self-sustaining, well, everything, had already existed in some lesser form of one kind or another throughout the world. We gathered them all together, picked the best aspects of each, reinvented every detail quite a bit, and improved upon their features in spades. Then, Eliza encoded large clouds of nanos to build them, while the rest of us worked with James Cooper and his crew in the building of the infrastructure of our then-new company, Pathway LLC, on Earth, before the formation of Pathway Industries. You were there, Vesha, but those memories may have faded, due to the dementia you were suffering from at the time. You now know or are relearning it all, but in quantities that are several orders of magnitude greater and in fractions-upon-fractions of a single second in time, and based upon our time dilation ratio, yet amenable to updates if we would wish to stay longer.*

That said, we finally dropped the reference to "LLC" or "Industries" and called our organization, Pathway. Everything you see was initially designed by Eliza and me. James helped us improve upon them, and together he and his crew helped us to make all of this happen. Believe me, Eliza thinks of everything. I helped a little bit, but you'd be amazed at how she thinks. We briefed every single one of Pathway's current population of more than two-billion citizens, fully, as soon as they were read-in, much like you now. Look over there."

Vesha suddenly felt her occipital lobe engage again, integrate with her vision, her hippocampus, her prefrontal cortex, and then connect from the corpus callosum. Vesha then discovered again that she now possessed what would be called, shared-thought, vision, and scope, and in this case, it was with Sky and Yesha, as she was now connected more deeply to their minds.

Vesha realized that her dominant and active cranial regions were coupled through each individual's corpus callosum to their dominant areas. Her visual ability multiplied exponentially zooming in to see extravagantly intricate details, down to the particles, then it scoped out again and she saw the fullness of the dark side of the Moon. It hovered within clear view, yet still gave way to the revelation of every finite detail.

Vesha and Sky were in fact seeing what Yesha was seeing. What left her even more impressed, were the waterfalls, the atmosphere that had an air of nature, calm, beauty, and a welcoming ambiance. Surrounding and within the tech cities, was cleanliness, colorful arrays of trees, forests, jungles, flowers, vegetation, morels, spices, and herbs of every kind. There were streams, and lakes, self-sustaining systems, and a unique melding of each aspect of nature with every single bit of the architecture of every building.

Vesha noticed how, although each building was unique, and in a magnificently beautiful way, they seemed to complement and integrate with each other and the nearby terrain with pristine quality and impenetrable durability. Each of the cities she beheld was connected in a variety of intuitive ways, beautiful to witness, and in its own intriguing manner—from the sky view of the city to the city's view of the sky and then the cosmos, itself.

Vesha drifted away, turned around and took advantage of the protection from the sunlight by the dark side of the Moon, to look at more of the constellations from the location she was at—she couldn't help herself, since she had done that as a professional all of her life.

There was Andromeda, the Milky Way's nearest major spiral galaxy, almost as clear as day. *"I can see her still there, coming closer, and she is beautiful. I can see better or more clearly than I ever did before, even with our country's most advanced telescopes. The stars, the constellations there, I can triangulate, and the physics that I know and am learning as I speak tell me there are quite a few fascinating planets that would be very nice to see soon. I'm hoping that 'someday' will be very shortly. Does this mean I am physiologically and neurologically upgraded with so much more than mere telescopic vision of a very cutting-edge variety?"*

"Yes, you are, and you can see her, Vesha. In every way, you are correct, it is due to telescopic vision, but that is one of the most advanced abilities along with one of the most difficult to learn, but you have learned it already, and I am proud of you. Your occipital lobe has been re-optimized, as well as your hippocampus, prefrontal cortex, corpus callosum, and the cornea, irises, pupils, and lenses of your physiological eyes. In the future, just like now, you will be able to engage these abilities as well as others you will be trained on, both inside and outside the Virtual Universe. Your hypothalamus and amygdala have been enhanced to maximize how your hippocampus processes everything and retain it, also adding to the enjoyment and appreciation of it all, as well as your ability to recall each of your memories as clearly and as soon as you need them. Andromeda is beautiful though, isn't she?"

Then Yesha turned slightly to her right, to continue her training and pointed as she spoke, *"What do you think of this?"*

Vesha turned and looked where Yesha was pointing and realized that she had again sent a mental image of what she was leading at from Yesha's viewpoint and location. Before her, on the conveniently located digital display, was all of the essential information.

Vesha then felt her mind fill with clarity and explained to Yesha's satisfaction what she saw, *"Just like a moment ago, I can see what you see right now, as if I were you, and I can study the intricate details of the Twelve Database Moons, but I've focused closer and can see their insignias and their ornate complexity, as well as the aesthetics of it all. Wow! Now I'm in awe of what they can do and what they hold within them. I am in fact receiving robust and phenomenal updates quickly. The speedy comprehension-levels, the clarity of the visual aspects of understanding, and the ability to derive and surmise so much based on just a few pages of what is available within my mind, courtesy of these Twelve Database Moons, has me in awe. I can fully understand the meaning for each symbol, all of which seems to be flooding into my mind as soon as I see it! You two were way ahead of many when it comes to robotics, nanos, and artificial intelligence!"* As the purpose behind each symbol became clear, so much more made complete sense, and then she was moved with emotion. *"Yesha, you should know that you, yourself, certainly deserve credit for lighting a fire under Eliza's innovative prowess. You have complemented her brilliance in every possible way. The closest friends I have, aside from my family that do that for me are Sky, Najem, and Jasmine.*

"Here I am, integrated with your and Eliza's minds, with Sky actually accompanying both of us as her own living entity, and this experience is through the roof—I'm trying not to cry! These symbols have quite a

history to them! It's as if they represent in visual form, a bit of artistry, the desire for peace among civilizations, and communication of the Universe. I can understand so much more, to include the breadth of the physical properties and abilities of these database moons. I can see where and when these images and symbols were communicated by the ancients of every dominant religion and civilization of Earth's latest historical inhabitants. I can see somehow that each of these was received through frequencies and other radiated communications and put into play as intended. Who would have known these symbols had a higher value of purpose than what we had initially appreciated or took them for? They integrate, as if cracking some long-lost and encrypted code. Everything symbolic is there, and it is all so elegant and so majestic. I can see cryptograms, including those of the ancient Egyptians, the Assyrians, the Muslims, the Norse Pagans, and each of the Asian and Hindu Religions. Oh, Christian faiths of all genres, Jewish faiths of each type, and intriguing religions I had no idea about before. I can see the Navajo, Cherokee, Aztec, Mayan, Pomo, Pygmy, Aborigine, and Eskimo faith symbols, and so many more, and the list goes on, are all woven in from all over our world. Wow! They seem to tie into the radiation reflective-absorption balance and defensive capabilities of the Database Moons themselves. I'm quite taken aback by the artistry and sophistication here. This is truly amazing, Yesha. Really! This is awesome. Who would have known?

"Wow!

"This is beautiful.

"I am actually quite impressed.

"How did you guys pull this off?" Vesha then saw the gigantic shield-like massive constructs protecting the Earth, Selene, and the database moons. It had never donned on her how much Eliza and Yesha had planned and then through James and his crew, they had carried out ever-so-brilliantly. She felt peace in her heart at the safety and security the people on Earth could move forward with, if only they knew. She saw how each shield around each planet throughout the solar system provided just the right amount of energy and light in intervals to each spherical surface, so as to protect them all, and in a unique way. The Moon, for example, was given the kind of protection necessary to afford it a beautiful, yet cozy atmosphere, and she saw where the terrain was actually teeming with rivers, lakes, mountains, cliffs, waterfalls, islands, seas, and life. However, if viewed from outside the Virtual Universe, no one would ever know this existed at all or at least in that way.

Yesha then explained, *"Eliza thought about all of this, a way to preserve our minds, a way to preserve our solar system, a way to preserve our home world, and even a way to connect from one being to another. Since the creation of these shields and database moons, as well as the creation of Pathway, we have melded minds with people from all over the world, and so many more forms of life than I will list at this time.*

"Vesha, there is a lot of purpose behind each symbol; simply put, these symbols have everything to do with the proper balance of absorption and deflection of radiation of every single kind of particle, to include both baryonic and non-baryonic material, and all as your mind has revealed to you and you have noted."

Yesha then pointed toward another location on what she now understood as an ancient planetary spheroid they occasionally called Selene, and Vesha saw, again, it was the Moon. There it was, the Moon, beautiful Selene, and she was teeming with wildlife, with spacious running areas for stampedes of buffalo, deer, elephants, lions, leopards, bears, tigers, and giraffe; every single animal a person could imagine was right there, together, healthy, happy, safe, full of life, and no longer wild, but tame, domesticated, and sentient. They were all out for a stroll, linking mind-to-mind, and they were looking out for one another with an intriguing sense of politeness. Gone was any reason for predation, and in its place was a collective-sense of well-being, with plenty of locations filled with viable food in a beautiful home they all shared.

There were mountains, rivers, streams, forests, oceans, islands, and even continents filled with beautiful, artistic, and futuristic tech cities that were beyond description in their beauty and usefulness. Spaceports were everywhere, with a wide variety of transportation options, and each with a vast array of purposes.

"Just like you see on Selene, the same is true on Mars, its moons, Ceres and other spherical asteroids or small planets, the moons and planetoids of the giant gas planets, Pluto and the dwarf planets of the Edgeworth-Kuiper Belt, and further out to the Oort Cloud and each of their moons, and any spherical planetoid throughout our solar system.

"As we rescue the refugees, those reared in abusive homes, victims of malevolence, tragedies, or natural disasters, and each person willing, once pre-trained at Pathway Campuses, they are then optimized physiologically and neurologically, and they enter the Virtual Universe, and are encouraged to share their wisdom. From there, they are given safe domicile in any of the tech cities you see, with resplendent luxuries and views that are breathtaking year-around!

"With all that I have shared with you, the more we collectively learn and train each other and with each other, the more the entire process of mastering our new abilities become more comfortable to control. When that happens, you will find that fewer advanced-control-mechanisms and maintenance algorithms by our space nanos are needed. This is due to the fact that our bodies

will, through this due diligence, emulate those abilities and adapt them to our own biological construct. In many ways this helps to preserve our humanity.

"Right now, as I have shared with you and Sky before, the total population of the tech cities is at two-billion citizens, and growing, so you can imagine that the collective wisdom in Pathway, via the Twelve Database Moons, shared by everyone here through the Virtual Universe, and continuously growing through our neural links, is exponential. No matter how connected we are, no matter how much we share, or how alike our overall goals may be, we still have, and always will have, our individuality and all of the beauty that comes with it.

"Now, you haven't asked, but many do, and there is something that it is important for you to know, and that is how all of this was financed. So, I will put this briefly, because of Eliza's designs, her creation of the nano cloud systems for each individual and each area of any determinate size throughout our solar system, and her innate ability to reinvest, while providing what is needed to increase the quality of life for everyone within Pathway, economically, Eliza's financial worth is in the one-hundred-Octodecillions as valued by the US Dollar.

"There is much more to explore, but we need to return soon to Eliza. We saw the tech cities, we've seen the sprawling landscape, but have you seen the extent of the Moon Base?" Yesha, beckoned her mentally to follow

her gaze, and there it was, another beautiful location with a seemingly infinite series of high tech, tall, and arching domes, also teeming with luscious forests, life, industry, productivity, and portals full of activity, with spacecraft entering and exiting the large spaceport. *"The science of all of this is quite exhilarating to consider, and all that you see is part of an advanced system protecting the life of our Sun for trillions of years and more. It is also still covert to the public eye. The people on Earth will be quite surprised when all of this is revealed, don't you think?"*

With that question, Vesha was again moved emotionally at how profound Eliza, Yesha, James, and all of Pathway had thought and prepared for countless possibilities that concerned so many. Considering how it was that humanity would no longer have need to worry about so many future events, other than the preservation of the local stellar region, the Milky Way, as well as all of the galaxies and the Universe itself, she agreed. *"With everything going on here, Yesha, I have no doubt the public and all of humanity will be quite surprised."*

Just like that, Vesha, Sky, and Yesha had returned and were instantly back on the couch, sitting beside Eliza, with her dog, Tyson, cuddled beside her as she listened to her music and meditated.

All of a sudden, Vesha felt as though her mind was linked to Eliza's, to all of her emotions, her dreams, her experiences, her knowledge, her wisdom—it all came flooding in. Unexpectedly, she could no longer speak.

It was as though Vesha was all of a sudden, a drifter, peering out, observing, feeling, and experiencing the life of Eliza Amber Williams—it was as if she was Eliza.

It felt new, it felt refreshing, inspiring, and more unique than anything she had ever felt before. The complexity of it all, the sweet flavor of individual thought and experience and perspective, was mesmerizing.

This was more surreal, yet real and delicious, to her mind than she had ever had the capacity to experience at any point within her mortal life. The same was true of her understanding, and she knew she would never be able to express what she was feeling in words once she returned to the real world.

Vesha began to grasp with complete clarity why it was that she needed to be trained within the Virtual Universe. This was the most beautiful treat of all, to link minds, and while she had linked minds in other beautiful and indescribable ways with Yesha, and while she had always been linked to Sky, who had been with her all of her life and still was, her own thoughts began to drift away, and she released the perceptions of her own mind, tearing away the misconceptions of perceived reality and she let go...

Appendix

Appendix – Character Summaries (Spoiler Alert)

Eliza Amber Williams – She is one of the primary characters in the Further than Before: Pathway to the Stars, two-part, and Pathway to the Stars series. After due diligence, she is awarded Doctorates in Mathematics, Physics, Quantum Theory, Biotechnology, Neuroscience, Psychology, and Law. She establishes Pathway LLC, grows it to become Pathway Industries, and later, simply Pathway. She writes a book, called Pathway to the Stars, forms and heads the UP, becomes a United States Representative for the State of Massachusetts in late 2016, is elected as a Senator for the US Senate in late 2018, and then wins the election twice and serves as the President of the US 2025-2033. She corrals the nations all over the world and establishes the United Allied States, in 2025, and is elected to serve a one-hundred-year term as UAS President. She also commissions Vesha Celeste to head the Intergalactic Mission Contingency, where she sets in motion the building of fourteen gigantic intergalactic spacecraft, twelve are IMC Zonal Command Spacecraft, one is the IMC Command Spacecraft, and one is the UAS Presidential Spacecraft. Eliza leads the way in an effort to preserve the Universe and with it all creatures who respect life. While living with quality, clarity, and a worthy legacy to share, evolution becomes a personal choice.

Yesha Alevtina – She is Eliza's best friend, the story's narrator, Eliza's Pathway VP, and she succeeds Eliza as the President of Pathway, from 2015-2022. She was born on July 1st of 1977, to Dr. Yesenia Alevtina, Ph.D. in Neurology, Physiology, and Psychology, and Dr. Stewart Alevtina, who passes away when she was two-years-old, in late 1979. Raised with Eliza, they become close friends.

She serves as Vice President of the US from 2025-2033, and as the US President from 2033-2041, with Joanne Gallant serving as the VP.

James Cooper – Serves as Eliza's right-hand-man. Born on July 9th of 1973, to Mr. and Mrs. Cooper, was raised with an excellent work ethic and a natural knack for high-level management. He worked for YY Construction Corporation until he was recruited by Eliza, as the third member of Pathway. As such, Eliza, Yesha, and James are the hierarchy of Pathway, the UP, and the pioneers of the technological advancements, the necessary infrastructure, and the leadership to usher in the Golden Age, where all of Earth-based civilization is brought in with clarity as to how they can contribute to further advancements while on missions, journeys, and quests. He buys out YY Construction Corp, renames it Pathway Construction, and absorbs it into Pathway. He is also of romantic interest to Eliza Williams, the Leader of the Golden Age.

Vesha Celeste – She is born in 1928 and has passed away as a beloved Astrophysicist and dear friend to Eliza and Yesha, two years later, she is the first human to be revived or reawakened after having taken her journey to the unknown on Christmas day of 2016. Two years later, after working with Eliza and many other Pathway citizens, Yesha revives her, and she begins her missions, journeys, and quests to explore the Universe, with the many preparations that come before it. She is appointed by UAS President Eliza Williams as the Commander of the Intergalactic Mission Contingency, responsible for the delivery of Twelve IMC Zonal Commands to their various areas of operation. Once complete, she will take her IMC Command Spacecraft and travel beyond the limits of the CMB as relative to Earth and Sol. Erin Carter serves as her Vice Commander. She is a close friend of Najem Grace and Jasmine Belle, both astrophysicists.

Amber Blythe – She is born in 1987, and raised with her sister, Sarah, who passed away at an early age due to many physiological complications, she decided early on that she would become a biogerentologist, a bioscientist, and an expert in physiology. With great goals, she is a major recruit by Eliza in the early days of Pathway LLC. She would go on to find a cure for Erin Carter, a young six-year-old girl, stricken with Hutchison-Guilford Progeria Syndrome. A prominent figure, she develops upgrades to Eliza's biopod machines that optimize both the physiology and the neurology of all who desire to live indeterminate lifespans, so they can either journey on long trips through the cosmos with the ability to return or stay behind but be there when family and friends return from their journeys. She serves as US President Eliza Williams' Press Secretary and is appointed to be the Commander of IMC Zone-04, with TJ Dmitry.

Erin Carter – She is born in 2004 and lived with Hutchison-Guilford Progeria Syndrome for the first six years of her life, yet she had an iron will, a graceful heart, and an unusually intelligent mind. Eliza, Yesha, and James sent Amber to work as a Delegate for Pathway on her first mission to rescue Erin and help her parents as well. As a result, she is optimized both physiologically and neurologically and is given an opportunity for even greater than the average life. She uses her newfound skills and abilities to rescue and help heal others. She grows up as a child prodigy and becomes one of the youngest and most prolific Presidents of her time. From 2018-2022 she serves as Yesha's Vice President and from 2022-2029 she serves as the President of Pathway. She is close to Amber, Joanne, Sky, and Vesha, and loves female vocal trance and is commissioned by UAS President Eliza Williams to serve as Vesha Celeste's Vice Commander on-board the Intergalactic Mission Contingency Command Spacecraft, with a secondary mission to fulfill once her duties with Vesha have been completed.

Matthew J. Opdyke

Sky, Vesha's Dream Angel – "Heal, don't harm," is her mantra. She goes on journeys with Vesha Celeste whenever Vesha goes to sleep and comforts her whenever she is lost in thought or daydreaming. Sky is one of Vesha's alter-egos, or the manifestation of individuality of different and powerful portions of the brain. She meets her in the Virtual Universe as a separate entity, which until then was the first time this had happened for the many individuals who had been trained within the Virtual Universe.

Najem Grace – She is born in 1925, Najem is biologically the oldest individual serving as a figurehead within Pathway and as an Intergalactic Mission Contingency Spacecraft and Zonal Commander. She became friends with Vesha Celeste and Jasmine Belle, through their shared interest in the stars and in space travel. As an astrophysicist, she was responsible for a lot of the legacy technologies through NASA and finally gets to see countless deep sky objects up close and personal. While introduced in the first book, she will resurface later on in the "Further Than Before" Series, in book three, as a major character, where we will learn more about her backstory and explore more of our Universe during her journeys through Zone-02.

Jasmine Belle – She is born in Northern Ireland in 1943, raised as a child in London, and eventually served alongside Najem in NASA, she is an astrophysicist and best friend of Vesha and Najem. Through her service and work with Pathway, she is appointed as an Intergalactic Mission Contingency Spacecraft and Zonal Commander, for Zone-01. We will learn more about her backstory, her missions with Pathway, and her journeys through the cosmos in book two of the "Further than Before" series.

Ralston Rayna – Vesha's husband, who passed away in 2008.

Daniel Rayna – Vesha's son, born in 1951. He has a Doctorate in Physics.

Jillian Yenn – Vesha's daughter, born in 1952, passed away after her battle with cancer in 2014. She had a Doctorate in Astronomy.

Chris Rayna – Vesha's son, born in 1956. He has a Doctorate in Mathematics.

Avery Rayna – Vesha's son, born in 1960. He has a Doctorate in Geology.

Matthew J. Opdyke

Appendix – Glossary

As a courtesy to the great minds of those who read this book or who have authored countless significant advances, the author has endeavored to list terms and acronyms introduced or used within this book in their fictional form. While this is not an all-inclusive list, the purpose of this glossary is to educate and inform while providing insight and further context to the story.

Antimatter – British physicist Paul Dirac won a Nobel Prize in 1933, essentially describing that all baryonic matter can carry an opposite charge, i.e., electron vs. positron, proton vs. antiproton, etc. When combined to form antimatter they behave similarly to ordinary matter. When antimatter and ordinary matter meet, they destroy or annihilate each other.

Baryonic Matter – All matter that you can currently interact with, within your natural state. According to established sciences, baryonic matter includes protons and neutrons, or more accurate, baryonic matter possesses a triquark configuration. In standard definitions, electrons are excluded, since they are classed as leptons. However, for the purpose of this text and subsequent texts in this literary series, this term is used more loosely to include electrons.

Bioenvironment – Any environment that enables a reasonably healthy life, in the case of Eliza or anyone on her team, this would provide an optimally healthy quality of life, which would augment both the physiology and neurology of organic and sentient organisms and beings.

Biopod – Biopods are pivotal to the story. Eliza finished the first prototypes in 2007 and improved upon them with Yesha. Eliza and Yesha were the first two to use them. James was the third to use one while going through his experiences with Eliza and Yesha. This machine is much like a glowing white perpendicular tanning booth, wherein you lay, it is comfortable, you shut the door, mentally state "1, 2, 3, 5, 20", in which 5 is an example of the quantity of real-world time your body lays in the biopod in terms of minutes, and 20 is an example of your life-like experience in the Virtual Universe time in terms of years.

This will interface you, if you so choose, with the Virtual Universe, and in it, not only will you be able to experience life, but you will also be able to interface with the Twelve Database Moons and connect mind-to-mind with others who are there or who have passed through it. You will also have an opportunity to study and improve upon newly acquired skills and abilities through educational pursuits, experiential-physiological feedback, free movement throughout any part of the terrain, where the only individuals you will see are those whom you are linked to neurologically and therefore, knowingly. In the Virtual Universe and individual can achieve complete mind-to-mind and neurological understanding.

Ultimately, when interacting with any other individual within the Virtual Universe, each person is bound by consent, such that, if they are within their own matrix, all rules are laid out, and a person entering that region will have a complete quickening of these rules and agree upon them if they continue within the other matrix for the duration they are there. Furthermore, an individual under the age of consent will only be able to see and interact with child-friendly subject matter and personalities.

Finally, a biopod is used to heal people both in body and mind, connect people to the Virtual Universe, and optimize any user both physiologically and neurologically.

Casimir Effect – In the story, this is used by Pathway and Eliza in the most robust, fantastical, and hypothetical of ways, especially in relation to control of attractive and repulsive forces. According to established sciences, in 1948, Dutch physicist Hendrik Casimir predicted that physical forces arise from a quantized field. He described this effect suggesting that the existence of conducting metals and dielectrics of one field revises the vacuum expectation value of the energy of a second quantized electromagnetic field. This plays a significant role in the chiral bag model, in relation to symmetry, fermions, and mesons and is used in cutting-edge microtechnologies and nanotechnologies.

Cold Fusion – In the story, this is the ability to separate electrons, protons, and neutrons into leptons, up quarks, down quarks, and their antimatter equivalents, and store them in a safe and stabilized state. The story even goes as far as including all forms of matter. This is done to later recompose them into fantasy molecules, as well as standard atoms and molecules without nuclear decay. Doing this assists Pathway's goals of providing a high quality of life free of danger to a life-friendly environment. Eliza and Yesha discover and use this process at micro and macroscopic levels, in December of 2007.

Commerce Matrix – Part of the Virtual Universe, explained in more detail in future books.

Correctional Matrix – Part of the Virtual Universe, explained in more detail in future books.

Cosmic microwave background (CMB) – Sometimes referred to as cosmic microwave background radiation, or CMBR, this is the limit of our ability to see Vesha furthest distance relative to our location, due to the speed of light, where the light source or information received comes from radiation known as microwaves. Currently, that location lays in a spherical radius at approximately forty-eight-billion light years from us, using math that includes the speed of light, the Doppler Effect, and the speed of the expansion as well as the time since the Big Bang. To be clear, under this theory all objects are moving away from each other, so it would reasonably be difficult to pinpoint the central location of this singularity.

Dark Energy – According to established cosmological and astronomical scientists, this is an as-yet very-little understood matter, or by-product of the kinetic energy of the Big Bang, that comprises approximately sixty-eight percent of the volume of energy in space. In the book, Vesha and Eliza discover the necessary properties that allow us to harness its power as well as the power of dark matter, pare it in a fantastical way to jump through space, and control the expansion, such that the Universe can expand and contract gently, like the lungs during the breathing of a sleeping baby. As this occurs, the Universe will become eternal and provide the energy necessary for the immortality of benevolent, sentient, and living beings.

Dark Matter – This was a subject talked about by numerous theoretical physicists, and astronomer Vera Cooper Rubin brought this to the foray through her diligent studies, dedication to the understanding of her Universe, and her will to share this information until true substance was brought to the idea of what it was precisely that bound galaxies, superclusters, and the most massive structures in the Universe, filaments, together. Dark matter comprises approximately 85% of the matter in the Universe and about 23% of its density. The majority of dark matter is composed of mostly non-baryonic matter.

Database Moon Archive – All information from Pathway and in all of recorded human history is stored here both in raw form as well as through abridged narratives created to expand clarity on any subject studied in as full of manner as possible. This archive also has multiple backups of genetic sequences for every species of land, air, or water creature. Furthermore, all who choose to have their information backed up in this way, can return to life in an optimized body similar to that of Vesha Celeste or Sky Taylor, upon their return from the dead, and when ready. This is where the Virtual Paradise exists for those who wish to take a break from reality and live in an imaginative fantasy of sorts but stay connected with all other people who are read-in, living or deceased.

Education Matrix – Part of the Virtual Universe, explained in more detail in future books.

Entertainment Matrix – Part of the Virtual Universe, explained in more detail in future books.

Health Matrix – Part of the Virtual Universe, explained in more detail in future books.

Jump Gate – In appearance, it is like a sizeable donut-shaped object, depending on size it stands between ten and twenty feet in diameter, serves as a portal for teleportation, and maximizes the inconceivable abilities of quantum entanglement in order to allow a user, multiple users, and/or luggage and supplies to transport from one point in the Universe to another in an instant. It is linked to the Twelve Database Moons and can be built and maintained using a cloud of nanos.

Nanos – These are highly sophisticated and reprogrammable, self-replicating and self-maintaining microscopic cold-fusion factory robots that can be programmed within the Virtual Universe with the benefits of time-dilation to optimize physiology, neurology, buildings, spacecraft, or any construct conceivable and inconceivable, and are capable of teleportation, as well as cell and micro-organism healing. These are the backbone of the Pathway tech cities, and deep space exploration and capabilities efforts, and are sometimes referred to as bio-nanos, neural-nanos, nano clouds, and nanosystems.

Matthew J. Opdyke

Neural identification – Every individual is truly unique, as such no two minds, human, creature, HBCI, or AI, alike, share the same expressions, personality, or character since their neurology and physiology are always wired a little differently or become that way due to factors of accumulated knowledge, experience, perspective, and resultant wisdom. Since that is the case, early on Eliza found a way to precisely identify shared thoughts from our own through a neurological identification code or a neural identification, and she made it impervious to hacking. With a neural identification, individuals are granted access to anything necessary within Pathway for the purposes and missions inherent within Universal Ethics. Every individual is allowed private regions of the mind for compartmentalization, and for personal and private thoughts. This right is protected, so long as actions expressed demonstrate that their minds are keeping within accordance of the principles of Universal Ethics (i.e., common sense: no murder, rape, emotional or physical abuse, no destruction of others' property, and no theft of others' gains made through honest diligence and intent).

Neurological Optimization – This is one of two structural upgrades to any living being who is optimized via a biopod or via an HBCI, like Sky Taylor. This upgrade is one that affords, at a minimum, an increase in the higher virtues of kindness, compassion, and empathy, as well as clarity of mind toward what one can do to advance civilization and improve upon a legacy worthy of preserving for the long-haul.

Primarily, a neurological optimization cures an individual of neurological disorders of any form, thereby allowing a person to enjoy life and appreciate others as well as themselves. Finally, an individual will have private or intimate thoughts protected within a specialized-compartmentalization of their brain, so long as they do not harm or cause undue consequence to the personal freedoms of others of life, liberty, and the pursuit of happiness, as well as consent. As time goes by anyone can learn countless skills, abilities, and a rich level of education and experiences with instantly-available recall and knowledge convergence when tackling issues.

Nobel Laureate – This is someone who has been a recipient of the Nobel Prize in any of a number of specific areas, from Physics to Philosophy. The Nobel Prize has been in existence since 1901, has been awarded on 585 occasions to 923 individuals and organizations. It is named after Swedish inventor, Alfred Noble. The idea is to recognize entities who have demonstrated outstanding achievements within the fields of literature, medicine, physics, chemistry, economics and activism for peace with one of the most prestigious awards.

Non-Baryonic Matter – In this book series, the author loosely coins this as material that, as far as we know now, we have no ability to touch, sense, or have an influence on. Think of every element on the Periodic Table, everything you can see, stars, galaxies, etc., and every particle that impacts our lives, like photons, quarks, and electrons, and so much more as baryonic matter, all else, such as dark matter and dark energy is non-baryonic matter. The correct definition of non-baryonic matter includes electrons, photons, and everything except triquark configurations, such as protons and neutrons. We can interact with most baryonic matter in large enough quantities and are limited only by our degree of advanced tools. Essentially, we can interact with 4.6% of the energy of the Universe. Please note that there are a variety of statistics, all with regard to energy and mass, dark matter comprises approximately 23% of the energy of the Universe and dark energy 72%.

Optogenetics – For the purposes of this book series, optogenetics is a method that uses light-sensitive proteins, called opsin, which may have had the most significant overall impact on the evolution of all creatures gifted with eyesight. This perhaps coincided with the development of occipital lobes, a system the brain uses to process visual information. Neuroscientists, such as Dr. Edward Boyden (who has taken the lead in neuroscience on overcoming issues such as Parkinson's and epilepsy), can conduct this non-invasive technique to understand and explore the mind more fully. Through this, they have developed a biological method that allows opsin to genetically modify the brain's neurons to effectively use light to control cells and living tissue and turn individual neurons or a region of them on or off.

Pathway – This is the organization founded by Eliza Amber Williams, officially, in 2008, beginning with three members as Pathway LLC, Eliza, Yesha Alevtina, and James Cooper. With all three at the helm, they build the infrastructure necessary to create and sustain life with benevolent sentience and they afford humanity the ability to eventually span the Universe, preserving life, connecting with other civilizations, and engaging in an honorable and shared purpose.

Pathway LLC becomes Pathway Industries in 2012, and not much later it becomes Pathway. All three are responsible for establishing the Universal Party and, together, they garner the support necessary to inspire all nations, globally, to form the United Allied States. Due to the brilliance of their groundwork, solar-system-wide, humanity eventually catches up through inspiration and clarity of mind and becomes ready to span the cosmos with an honorable legacy to share, of a unique and common goal, to preserve the life of the Universe.

Pathway Convention Center – The primary physical location in the US, used to conduct massive real-world meetings and training. This large location is more significant in size than publicly understood or known and is several football stadiums combined in size, in the real-world portion of the complex. People who are not read-in can drive and park in a massive undercover parking facility using valet service. Those who are read-in can use the hyperloop system and jump gates to arrive there. This center is attached to a vast dormitory for visitors and refugees, where each domicile is more luxurious than a penthouse suite in the most expensive hotels worldwide. This system is linked to labs and other immense facilities within the Melrose, Massachusetts, Campus, and globally.

Pathway Covert Campus – Systems like these are located within many areas of the world and throughout the solar system. Each campus is connected through a series of hyperloops and jump gates. This is where the most technologically advanced breakthroughs are made and protected, prior to dense-regional proliferation to the furthest reaches of the globe and the solar system.

Physiological Optimization – This is one of two structural upgrades to any living being via a biopod or an HBCI, like Sky Taylor. This upgrade is one that affords, at a minimum, being cured of any and all physiological and neurological ailments, diseases, or complications. Any recipient who receives the full set of optimizations is granted a Pathway citizenship, and with it, the abilities for controlled and heightened senses. Additionally, they will find their cells have rejuvenated to where their physique is as remarkable as they would have imagined it being, where they are as an optimized twenty-two-year-old. As any individual learns and uses their new skills, i.e. telescopic, microscopic, and all other types of vision needed at any given time, their powers increase and multiply, and are retained indefinitely. However, if a person demonstrates ill-will toward others, they will begin to return to their natural state and age like normal. By going through the Correctional Matrix, these benefits can be regained.

Quantum Computing – For the purposes of this book, a quantum computer helps to determine any best course of action in split seconds. This deterministic tool allows for time dilation to be used when interfaced with and within the Virtual Universe, where individual particles and wavelengths of radiation of every variety can be manipulated for the benefit of life. As it is described throughout further parts of the story, there are many amazing things that can be done, courtesy of quantum computing.

In the real world, quantum computing is a system that can provide calculations based on quantum bits, or qubits. It is a system that uses entanglement to offer both 0s and 1s, or neither, or one or the other, and the resultant effect is indeterminate unless the beholder takes advantage of each state of quantum entanglement.

Quantum Entanglement – In this sci-fi-fantasy series, this is a mechanical marvel at a particle level and smaller in scope, but it is every bit as powerful when it comes to what it is that we can do, if given the right tools. A fuller understanding of this is intriguing, however, using this for purposes within the scope of the principles of Universal Ethics allows us a beautiful Universe full of possibilities, wherein the quantum conditions of two or more entities can be described with reference to the other, and even though the separate entities may be spatially separated using the correct mechanisms, they can be manipulated.

Quantum Sensor or Sensor – These sensors are the primary intelligence gathering devices of all Pathway Spacecraft, among other purposes, and they are used to travel from point-to-point anywhere throughout any relative and observable Universe.

Real world – "Real world", i.e. 'the real world,' or "real-world," i.e., in 'real-world politics' (grammar dependent), both are used in this story redundantly and in this way to differentiate between what is known and proliferated in a public environment from what is developed and improved upon with Pathway eyes only.

Red Blood Cells – These cells play a vital role in our health by cycling fresh oxygen throughout our bodies, and, our blood consists of between forty to forty-five percent of these critical cells. About 2.4 million new erythrocytes are made each second in human grownups.

Smartsuit – A suit used from 2008-2022 by many in Pathway that worked as an all-in-one for wardrobe holo-imagery, hygiene, and added protection from the harsh elements in outer space and even on Earth. Around 2010, an option is given to enter a biopod using everyday attire, rather than using a smartsuit, and in doing so, the biopod would be able to convert their clothes into a smartsuit. This intriguing tech revolves around a connection that is exclusive to an individual's neural identification, using a distinct compartment within the mind to apply a standard and individually-paired set of wardrobes for any given occasion and is useful in its unique relation to the user's personal creativity, whims, and desired features. This tech eventually allows fashion designers to sell individual, unique, and tailored wardrobes all encoded explicitly for each user. Further upgrades will be explained in later books within any associated series.

Stem Cells – These types of cells are unique, in that, at the time of cell division they can become any type of tissue, cell, or organism. Sources of stem cells include bone marrow, fat tissue, and blood donations. Adult stem cells can mend any type of tissue and can be turned into somatic cells, using white blood cells as the vehicle to arrive to the proper destination, based on physiological and neurological need and communication. Embryonic stem cells can divide and become any tissue, organ, nerve, or cell, and likewise travel through the body, in a white blood cell nucleus. Embryonic cell lines and autologous embryonic stem cells generated through somatic cell nuclear transference or dedifferentiation are promising candidates for future therapies.

Supercluster – This is a grouping of galaxies bound by gravity, all existing in the same Filament. (Please see definition for filament)

Telomerase – This is a natural enzyme that helps to grow the length of the caps at the ends of our genes, called telomeres. They prevent cellular damage and senescence. Astragalus root has been identified as an organic resource for telomerase and is a naturally and organically available part of the pea family growing in the northern and eastern parts of China. Telomerase therapy is a promising method for rejuvenating cellular health. Studies are still being made for the useful introduction of this enzyme into colonies of cells to mitigate cellular senescence.

Telomere – The caps at the end of our genes that shorten as our cells divide throughout our lives, and as they shorten, or become too short, our cells become senescent, we begin to show the signs of the disease called aging, and we become susceptible to cancer, heart failure, lung failure, dementia, diabetes, or other life-threatening physiological complications. It is to our benefit to find a way to lengthen our telomeres. Our cancer cells already have, and if it weren't for them killing their host, they would live forever. If we could remove this from, or repurpose, our cancer cells it is likely that we could make it possible for our healthy cells to produce telomerase, and we could theoretically live forever.

Twelve Database Moons – A single database moon is approximately three-hundred miles in diameter with robust capabilities of every imaginable sort. Some of its abilities include the use of invisibility, renavigation, magnetic and repulsive technologies for all types of matter, frequencies, and radiation as desired to protect life, preserve it, and for self-maintenance. In total, as suggested, there is a network of twelve of them orbiting the Earth, a safe distance beyond the orbit of the Earth's Moon, working congruently with the invisible shielding protecting the Earth and the Moon from any sort of malady that would compromise the ability for these biospheres to sustain life.

Each of these database moons has multi-functional capacities, from data storage to the highest tech satellite capabilities and the ability to ensure all communication and transportation can be instantaneous using jump gates and other forms of teleportation. There are many other unexplained capabilities, but they will surface further along within any associated series.

They redundantly store all types of data, up to and including every matrix of the Virtual Universe, and this includes the Paradise Matrix—a place to go to rest for a given period of time, also, as yet to be introduced in further-associated-series. It carries a backup of every creature's and consenting human's deoxyribonucleic acid, or DNA, genetic and neurological identification, and all associated memories, as well as a robust system to protect and preserve all of life, the solar system, and itself.

Universal Ethics – Simply put, Universal Ethics as established by the United Allied States consists of preservation of life, increasing the quality of life, creating diplomatic bridges and solutions, honoring personal consent, not causing undue consequence to the rights of others, multiplying the capacity of the mind with clarity, beginning with kindness, finding a way to contribute to the overall advancement of civilization, and building a legacy worthy of preserving for the long-haul.

Universal Ethics recognizes there is untold and untapped potential in every living being. By truly understanding one another and working together we can advance further until we can preserve the life of the Universe itself, allowing it to breathe, gently causing subtle expansion, retraction, and repeating that cycle continuously, thereby gifting the Universe the ability to preserve life indefinitely. As advancements and exploration continues on to strengthen and advance our Universe even further, we simultaneously advance to other Multiverse systems, meeting the same ethics of well-being, health, longevity, and clarity of mind over greed and power, where everlasting joy is gained through wisdom, compassion, and innovation with the intent of well-being for others as well as ourselves. The longer we live in a healthy manner, the more we can compound upon our wisdom and the joy that comes from solutions to issues—and, together—all issues, whether great or small.

Universal Party or UP – The UP is founded by Eliza Amber Williams, in late 2008. Its core values are based on Universal Ethics. The UP is a positive, motivational influence, allowing every citizen a valuable and viable say in governance, with pure democracy made available via conveyances provided in the Virtual Universe solar-system-wide, and for the purposes of this current story it is implemented within each of the tech cities. The UP was established in the US in 2010. Further development and successes will be explained as the story progresses.

Utopia – "No place" – Seeing the unattainable ideals toward raising the quality of life, increasing healthy and youthful longevity, and magnifying the clarity of mind, and creating an environment that can indefinitely sustain those ideals, Eliza decides to buck the impossible and make great things happen, despite the odds against her.

White Blood Cells – As possibly oversimplified and used in the text for the purposes of fiction, story-arch and plot, white blood cells are an essential part of our body's immune system. While there are a diversity of groups and subgroups of white blood cells, as a whole, they make up only one percent of our blood volume. As little as that percentage is, they originate from the marrow and serve to attack infections throughout the entire body. One subgroup, lymphocytes, consists of B, T, and NK cells. Of late, T cells have been studied for possible therapies that might pose positive for cancer treatment and cures. Much is necessary for these studies, still, but ultimately, positive outcomes are contingent upon cell-to-cell flow, communication, et al, for a massive revolution of cures for countless diseases, as well as physiological rejuvenation and upgrades.

Appendix – Artwork & Inspiration

1. "A Walk through the Virtual Universe" courtesy of Rikta Design, Artistic Credit: Tarik Sulić, Handover Contract: 302574, https://www.freelancer.com/u/RiktaDesign
Description of artwork according to artist: "Vesha Celeste gazes at a beautiful tech city and into the Cosmos while making her way through a portal to another place within the Solar System."

2. "Witchead Nebula" courtesy of NASA, Image Credit: NASA/STScI Digitized Sky Survey/Noel Carboni, https://www.nasa.gov/multimedia/imagegallery/image_featur e_1209.html, Description according to NASA: As the name implies, this reflection nebula associated with the star Rigel looks suspiciously like a fairytale crone. Formally known as IC 2118 in the constellation Orion, the Witch Head Nebula glows primarily by light reflected from the star. The color of this very blue nebula is caused not only by blue color of its star, but also because the dust grains reflect blue light more efficiently than red. A similar physical process causes Earth's daytime sky to appear blue.

Author Inspired by the writings and studies of:
Michio Kaku, Lisa Randall, Sam Harris, Thomas Paine, Ron Chernow, Juan Enriquez, Steve Gullans, Alec Ross, Liz Parrish, Michael Fossel, Aubrey de Grey, C.S. Lewis, Jennifer Doudna, Vera Cooper Rubin, Nancy Grace Roman, Jocelyn Belle Burnell, Daisey Robinton, Carl Sagan, Nikola Tesla, Albert Einstein, George Orwell, J.R.R. Tolkien, George R. R. Martin, James S. A. Corey, George Lucas, Ronald D. Moore, Glen A. Larson, Michael Taylor, David Weddle, Bradley Thompson, Michael Angeli, Anne Cofell Saunders, Carla Robinson, Gene Roddenberry, Harlan Ellison, David Gerrold, D. C. Fontana, Theodore Sturgeon, Jerome Bixby, Norman Spinrad, Robert M Sapolsky, Abraham Maslow, Leonard Wibberley, Sidduhartha Mukherjee, R. Buckminster Fuller, Michael Withey, Paulo Freire, Orson Scott Card, Eunsun Kim, Ashlee Vance, Ian Ridpath, Arthur W. Toga, John C. Mazziotta, Brian Greene, Benjamin Graham, Travis Bradberry, Jean Greaves, Dan Hooper, Kim Shumway, Jason Rothenberg, and of course, Douglas Adams and many others

Appendix – Bio of Author

Matthew J. Opdyke was born in Stanford University Hospital, California, and adopted at the age of nine. With loving parents who mentored, coached, and trained him, life for Matthew became filled with hope and wonder. Working hard, studying, playing after chores were done, and becoming an Eagle Scout further tempered his young character. He lived in Uruguay for two years, serving as a missionary for a wonderful church, and meeting many wonderful people there.

With great respect for the past, yet moving on, he found himself as an author for futuristic science fiction and fantasy novels and books that edify and inspire, after retiring from the military with seventeen years of service. Having served in several extra duties and having learned Spanish and some Indonesian, he learned to love the people of this world ten times over. Shortly after meeting his wife, he was finally able to buckle down and finish his Bachelor of Applied Science in Management, at Peru State College, in Nebraska. Since his youth, Matt has worked at a youth worker at Scout camp, in pear sheds, for retail companies, financial service companies, for a telephone company, construction companies, sheet-metal shops, various odd jobs, served in the US Air Force, to protect, rather than harm, and he has witnessed amazing leadership and in some instances where the revolving door was the hallmark, to say the least.

As he pored through biotechnology, neuroscience, and theoretical physics books galore Matt began to ask why he hadn't heard about this or that before, especially if it could help so many. Matt then developed a story arch and breathed life into numerous characters for his very first series of books tackling some of the intriguing questions of the day, and allowing it to take place in a less than ideal environment, much like what we experience daily, while also creating a future that we could all hope for and can attain, if we but read, become curious, inventive, and inspire each other, by recognizing the best within each of us. His main refrain is, "be kind, always."

Space Opera Novelist Matthew J. Opdyke is moved by our beautiful Universe and all that it has to offer. He seeks to display a confident, noble, and inspiring message throughout his writings to the masses of our vast civilization. Encouraged for many years by those who teach, lead, and mentor others in a manner that fosters innovation, he endeavors to imbue the main characters of his novels with many unique traits that lead to individual empowerment, as well as overall well-being and meaningful purpose, despite background or environmental influences. We can transcend from here with a belief in the preservation of life, our world, and every life-giving system we know throughout humanity. From our phenomenal world, Earth, to our Moon, the planets orbiting our Sun, to the distant stars and the complexity of their networks, Matthew J Opdyke has been curious about the sciences that govern their existence and strengths for decades. Within these sciences lie the tools that will help us to safely and, in some cases, dangerously and daringly explore it all!

He often asks, how can we brave the effects of interstellar radiation, so we do not die from its exposure? How can we travel without gravity, so our skeletal structures do not become too porous and cause our frames to be too weak to carry our weight? How can we mimic the effects of gravity, to allow humanity to explore outer space for long periods while maintaining strength and clarity of mind? There are so many questions to ask, and there are many answers. Some answers are considered the "hard truth" based on what we know today. Many ideas seem so far from reality, and they are considered the fantasies of the mad. Other answers dare to explore possibilities, imagine scenarios, and write about how humanity can cope in its earnest desire for long-term survival, as we begin to span the Cosmos.

Our Earth is beautiful, and until now, we can only make highly intellectual guesses as to whether or not this is a genuinely unique setting throughout the entirety of our Universe. Are we the only sentient humanoids (or any "-oid" for that matter), in existence? Is our Earth the only place that can sustain life, allowing the living to walk freely without overmuch harmful effects? Are there other places that allow evolution to take place gifting its inhabitants with sentience? If so, do they evolve like many within our world to have a desire to continue to exist? Do they care for other beings quite different from their own?

Given what we understand about physics, matter, and all that we can currently control, manipulate, and use, a lot of what we do for the benefit of both ourselves and those around us allows for the certainty that other worlds much like ours can exist, teeming with life. Can we meet these other civilizations? If we do, will we be able to survive together? How can that be possible? One of the most significant ways to achieve a shared understanding and set of goals is through effective communication, but what if we run into a world of dinosaurs? Will we be able to effectively communicate with them before being swallowed? If we could accomplish this form of relaying positive messages back and forth with well-being at the core, could we also achieve something that equates to shared purpose?

What is the one thing that all of life may fear, once they know about it? Is the "deep freeze" or the vast expansion of the Universe a threat to us all? What can we learn about our Universe to tame what rules it to save it? If we desire to work together to achieve this, will we need to become well-versed in all types of particles and matter, from dark matter to dark energy, and everything else from baryonic to non-baryonic? What can we do to successfully share our legacy with other civilizations while we learn about theirs? What terrors await us that we can scarcely fathom now? What promise awaits us if we dare to discover more? What could sentience be in comparison to the limits we know in our grand spiral galaxy, versus galactic clouds, elliptical galaxies, and a host of others? How would their environments affect their psyche? What kinds of life can live in the hotter regions that lie within the globular clusters of stars or near the black hole?

Many questions lie at the precipice of humanity's promise toward the future, and these questions are those that Matthew J Opdyke dares to entertain. Enjoy each character in his stories, with science fiction, fantasy, and space opera imbued into each booklet, book, and novel. Sometimes he dares to stick to the rules, sometimes he dares to be the mad and deranged lunatic, and at other times he dares to be creative and imaginative to come up with solutions to the issues that affect us today so that we can move forward tomorrow. Read, listen, and dare to dream!

Appendix – Published Works

Audiobooks:
Further Than Before: Pathway to the Stars, Part 1
https://adbl.co/2JLxTDf
Pathway to the Stars: Part 1, Vesha Celeste
https://adbl.co/2weOffT

Further than Before: Pathway to the Stars
Part 1: https://smile.amazon.com/dp/B07HL767WZ
Part 2: https://smile.amazon.com/dp/B07HL7F78F
Further Than Before: Parts 1 & 2 Together:
TOME: https://smile.amazon.com/dp/B07MCDP3PN

Pathway to the Stars
Part 1, Vesha Celeste: 978-1726768528
https://smile.amazon.com/dp/B07J2S8LLV
Part 2, Eliza Williams: 978-1729030301
https://smile.amazon.com/dp/B07JK5RD2N
Part 3, James Cooper: 978-1729495131
https://smile.amazon.com/dp/B07K2B5WS3
Part 4, Universal Party: 978-1798511374
https://smile.amazon.com/dp/B07P76VWLP
Part 5, Amber Blythe: 978-1799281108
https://smile.amazon.com/dp/B07PKCHTG4
Part 6, Erin Carter: 978-1091095427
https://smile.amazon.com/dp/B07PXHJ82N

A Cosmic Legacy: From Earth to the Stars:
https://www.amazon.com/dp/1733313125

Appendix – Thank you

Kim thank you for your insight, your inspiring ideas, and your support every step of the way. Thank you to the parents that adopted and raised me with love and wisdom. May they rest in peace. Thank you to all the heroes who have gone before, and who are no longer with us today, because of their bravery to save those they loved or others who they saw barely living in unjustifiable forms of misery and suffering. Thank you to the many scientists, philanthropists, selfless and truly dedicated teachers who mentor and coach, engineers, creative minds, and data-crunchers, I thank each of you for your never-ending and positive impact on so many, and even on me throughout my life. To the musicians and artists, your music and art inspires the mind and makes thinking possible in a great way. Listed or not, I appreciate art in so many forms.

To all my family and friends, thank you for being upbeat, spending many waking hours pushing my books, getting the word out, providing positive reviews, and overall being kind, loving, and supportive throughout the years. I thank you for listening to me go on about astronomy, biology, economics, management, neuroscience, physics, politics, and so much more until you were blue in the face. The heroes in life among the scientists, the revolutionary longevity science buffs and pioneers, neuroscientists, the theoretical physicists, astronomers, engineers, and legal titans all contributed in your own way.

Ultimately, if we want to get on that pathway to the stars, we all need each other, so, whatever we do, the first step toward a long-term legacy, and one we can embrace and be proud of, begins with simple kindness and love for others. As we search for purpose and meaning in our lives, I believe we will find it in the pursuit of well-being, longevity, quality of life, clarity of mind, and innovation

Matthew J. Opdyke

that has an end in preservation of life and bringing life and beauty to places once thought uninhabitable.

Matthew J. Opdyke, Author
For questions, please email:
info@mjopublications.com
https://www.mjopublications.com
https://smile.amazon.com/author/matthewopdyke

Appendix – Farewell for Now

I look forward to hearing from each of you and appreciate any constructive feedback. Please know that this message is intended to be uplifting, thought provoking, and of the most relevant and important you'll have the opportunity to read and pass on to others. Its focus is on long-term survival of not just our civilization but each of us, you included. If you were moved in anyway by the stories within, please know that your positive review on Amazon, Audible, Goodreads, Barnes & Noble, or any online bookstore will certainly help. Furthermore, if you feel inspired to invent or develop anything based on the technologies shared, feel free to simply email me at info@mjopublications.com, and with your permission I will share it on my personal blog. Reading this story and arriving at this juncture means that you are someone who indeed cares about the future of humanity, so therefore, I thank you! Regardless of what I have written, you are defined by you alone and no one else. It's up to us to decide what guides us in life, our ethics, our morals, and more.

Farewell for now...
Very Respectfully,

Matthew James Opdyke

www.ingramcontent.com/pod-product-compliance
Lightning Source LLC
Chambersburg PA
CBHW021156110726

47900CB00002B/604